I0451960

WULFGARD

THE TOMB
OF
ANKHU

DJEDAR RATH: BOOK I

Maegan A. Stebbins

Set in the world of Wulfgard, created by
JUSTIN R.R. STEBBINS
& MAEGAN A. STEBBINS

ISBN-13: 978-1-949227-03-1

Cover art by Justin R. R. Stebbins
Scene dividers by Maegan A. Stebbins

Visit Wulfgard and the author online at:
www.wulfgard.net
www.maverickwerewolf.com

CONTENTS

Empire of
Kemhet

Waset

Swenet

Ruins of
Urukkad

River Yter

Red Sands of
Deshret

Kas

Digsite

Axa

Zurtuum

Shulua

THE BLASTED
WASTES

TEFNAHKT'S
FORTRESS

BLEMMYES

PART I

Destruction.

Citizens gathered before the approach of a great temple where statues of the gods once overlooked every aspect of their lives. Those statues had been torn down and hacked to pieces, their stones scattered across the city. Many of the colorful hieroglyphs along the base of such statues had been slashed through and otherwise defiled, their images broken, while only desolate feet stood where mighty monuments were meant to sit or stand.

Now came a new ruler: one who did not tolerate effigies of this land's ancient and still-reigning gods, nor of the many pharaohs who had come before him: he who defied the sacred order of all things, including the duties of Men to maintain balance and the natural cycle itself.

Down the middle of the streets marched a procession of men and horses. A chariot gilded in gold and jewels, pulled by the most beautiful of steeds wearing attires of precious metals and gems, rode in the center of the army. The wealth on the chariot alone may have amounted to more value than the accumulated possessions of every conquered soul in the crowd.

The chariot came to a halt at the far end of the cowed audience, and the man who drove it stepped out before his people. He was tall and elegant, with a face like chiseled stone, his every severe feature rivaling those of the nearby toppled statue of the god Osiris. He wore only some robes about his waist and gold ornaments around his arms and neck and ankles, freely showing much of his body. The form of a living god was something to be eternally admired... though Ankhu's sinuous muscles and prominent veins hardly held the majesty of the perfect-bodied statues his soldiers had destroyed.

The people did not cheer for him. Silence spread across the crowd as Ankhu stepped up to a pedestal, one hastily erected by his warriors for such an occasion.

Speeches were for weak men, however. Ankhu gave no speech. He stood and looked out across his latest conquest, needing no words to prompt all those before him to kneel. Men, women, and children under his stare lowered themselves to their knees, bowing until their noses touched the earth. They swore loyalty – and swore to fear him, as he commanded of all under his rule.

But still there were those who did not fear.

As he looked over his subjects, one of his own warriors lunged with sword in hand. Barely three feet separated them, giving the soldier an easy opportunity to stab his long-time ruler in the back and at last defeat Pharaoh Ankhu the Endless, God-King, Demon-Sired, High Priest of the Black Temple and oppressor of Kemhet.

Ankhu kept his gaze forward, looking out at the people. He would not even regard the man who dared stand against him. With but a wave of his hand, the soldier fell to his knees, dropping his sword and crying out in pain. Slowly, Ankhu turned to face the soldier as he suffered, clutching at his chest, his soul writhing within him.

Ankhu said to the denizens of the conquered city, "Gaze upon this man. He is one of your own neighbors who turned traitor to serve me in my conquest of your home. Now, he raises his sword against me: a pitiful, mundane weapon." Ankhu did not kneel to pick it up, as Ankhu knelt for nothing. Instead, he gestured to another soldier, who ran over and scooped up the fallen blade, bringing it to his pharaoh.

Ankhu took it – and then, with but a glance, turned it to dust that blew away in the desert wind.

"No weapon can harm me," said Ankhu. "No mortal can end the reign of Ankhu the Endless." He looked out across his latest conquest – and scoffed. "When he joined my forces, this man begged me to show mercy. He pleaded with me that I might spare your homes, your

families, your souls. And so I did, for I can be merciful...
But now, his actions have forfeited all your lives."

Terror spread through the crowd before him. While
some knelt frozen in confusion and fear, others began
to scramble. They hoped to escape or at least hide, or
even to reach the nearest horse and set off in a random
direction into the mercy of the desert. Compared to
Ankhu, even the bleakness of the dunes seemed
welcoming.

Once again Ankhu lifted a hand, and from it flowed
power unspeakable. Within moments, the skies began
to blacken. A dark, swirling mass blotted out the sun –
and then descended upon the city.

They were insects of hell – swarms of them – a
plague never meant to be seen by Men. They would
devour all in their path: flesh and bone, animal and crop,
and their touch would spread a pestilence that could not
be identified nor cured.

Such was the will of Ankhu.

Now, the will of Ankhu was all but forgotten.
Eventually, the Endless found his end.

Over the course of untold years, perhaps even
thousands or more, Ankhu's reign fell into ambiguity.

Statues of his might erected by the empire he had built were since torn down or otherwise defaced by his former subjects. The passing of ages had its way of erasing or distorting history. If anyone short of a truly learned scholar did know Ankhu's name, they knew him only as an ancient evil pharaoh and little more than a legend...

But one ancient order remembered everything.

Those whose oaths bound them to preserve such history and to remember the greatest of evils above all else were now the only force standing between past and present – standing in the face of history repeating itself. They were the order known as the Medjai.

Or so legends claimed. Not that the slaves working in the middle of the desert would know.

Day had long since passed into night, and like every night, the master kept the slaves working. None would dare defy Tefnahkt the Red, owner of every slave present. But one slave's time to rest had come at long last.

Djedar Rath finally dropped his well-worn pick. Even after being driven for so many years under the same orders and whips, this felt exceptional. So much as fetching a drink resulted in harsh glares and reminders to get back to work, especially for him.

Heavy arms aching and sore, Djedar finally left behind the secluded little chamber he had chosen as his personal project. The dig site where he and the other slaves worked seemed so vast they could never uncover it all, and new walls were discovered every day. They had been given orders to search every chamber for an entrance into some mysterious, larger complex. The order had been issued a week or more ago, and despite working every day and night since, they'd found nothing but more dust-coated walls and obelisks colored in hieroglyphs. Master Tefnahkt the Red was growing impatient.

False doors dotted every ruin they tried to enter. Empty rooms stood everywhere, leading to nothing. So far, they hadn't found a way inside whatever greater structure rested deep beneath the sands. The room in which Djedar had worked all day was yet another pointless chamber, every wall lined in symbols and other sandy, almost worn-away images he hadn't yet deciphered.

Cold night wind chilled the sweat covering Djedar's almost naked form as he stepped into the open desert air, making him shiver. Other slaves continued to work in the light of the tall torch poles and braziers scattered over the massive dig site, but Djedar's time was done – at least for tonight. He didn't speak to any of them, stalking through the various projects toward one of the many camps where slaves were allowed a few hours of rest.

He passed by the current center of interest in the dig site: a treasure room, a chamber locked away behind bars golden in hue but sturdier than true gold – or any other metal they'd ever known. Warnings on the wall told of how the treasure was cursed and never to be disturbed; Tefnahkt, of course, did not care. The slaves worked there day and night, though Djedar was not allowed to do so, for fear he would sabotage the efforts due to being a 'traitor.'

Apparently, something in the room was structurally unsound. Djedar always kept his ears open, and he overheard a slave-driver shouting orders to the workers to be careful digging in the chamber, as an integral support pillar had weakened and could collapse at the smallest provocation. Interesting, but not of any importance. Not to him. All he wanted was sleep.

But as he prowled past groups of slave-drivers and armed guards, Djedar paused. Some of Tefnahkt's men had gathered not far from his resting place. One nudged a sleeping old man with the butt of his spear.

"Get up," the slave-driver ordered. The old man barely stirred, letting out a confused sound, half a cough and half a groggy grunt. "Get up!" the slave-driver repeated.

Djedar approached, though he stood just beyond the reach of the nearest torch's light. "Enough," Djedar said, drawing their collective glares. He didn't balk. "He's been sick for days."

"Sick or no, he's slept for six hours now," the slave-driver retorted.

"Do you really expect a sick old man to work this time of night?" Djedar asked calmly.

His interruption drew attention away from the elderly slave, who huddled in his blankets, pulling them over his splotched, bald head. Djedar didn't so much as glance his way, keeping his eyes trained on the slave-driver who turned toward him.

"If he's too sick and old to work," said the slave-driver as he took a step nearer, long whip dangling from one hand, "tell me why we shouldn't throw him out in the desert and let him start walking. Tefnahkt the Red doesn't waste food on the weak."

Djedar didn't miss a beat. "Tefnahkt the Red also doesn't waste slaves. You don't give the orders here." He lifted his head higher, looking down his face at the guard. "I'll take his place for the night."

The man barked out a laugh. "Taking the place of a dying old man, are you? Fine. You'll work his shift, and we'll let the useless sod take your sleep." He nodded back to where Djedar had come from. "Go."

With that, Djedar left. Every throbbing muscle in his body asked him why he would be so stupid. Why would he work himself to the bone even more than the masters demanded already? But he was beyond caring. Besides, he had a personal project to continue.

Making a beeline through the dig site once more, he returned to the same chamber, taking up a shovel and an oil lamp from beside the entrance. He ducked low under the half-broken doorway before rising to his full height again in the secluded room that led nowhere.

If he didn't have work to show the next slave-driver who checked on him, he would be punished for it. Whipped, most likely. For now, however, Djedar put aside his other tools, carrying the lamp to look along the walls again.

He couldn't read all that incredibly well, being a mere slave essentially all his life, but he'd seen enough buildings and scrolls to teach himself a few things. Stealing the occasional text for himself also helped. Familiar symbols dotted the walls, but they only seemed like sections of the full story.

Depictions of the Old Kingdom gods lined all sides of the chamber: the many animal-headed deities of Kemhet, the Black Lands – Djedar's homeland, where little had changed even since the time of these ancient ruins. Falcon-headed god Horus the Younger worked alongside the fearsome lion-headed goddess Sekhmet as they subdued a man who wore the royal headdress, the *nemes*, like the gods themselves to indicate his divine status as pharaoh.

The first images had been scraped off the wall. The second showed the divinities putting the pharaoh in black chains to bring him before the god Anubis, judge of the dead, a deity depicted as a man with the head of a black wolf. Presiding also was Set, god of chaos – but why would Set be there?

What story did they tell?

"Rath!" another of the slaves, one who often wanted to gossip, called from the half-collapsed doorway to his left. In the corner of his eye, Djedar saw a dark shape with a familiar face look in at him. "Are you alright? Why're you still working?"

"I like working," Djedar answered lightly. That wasn't true, of course.

"Weren't you digging in here all day already? Why do you dig in there, anyway? Looks like it could collapse on you any second."

Talking so much would draw attention to them. "I guess it could. It's very exciting." Djedar flashed the man a quick smile. "What're *you* doing?"

The other slave scoffed, shaking his head and leaving. Flippancy usually had a way of sending off annoyances. Djedar returned to work, running his fingers along the walls, searching for any lever or button. He paused occasionally to knock the flat of his pick against the stone, listening for hollow openings behind the facade.

His curiosity went unrewarded. The chamber was a dead end. Every wall stood thick and sturdy, hiding nothing, and deterioration destroyed the colorful stories the stones once told. Still he had only the partial tale about the strange pharaoh the gods themselves put in black chains and, seemingly, judged before his mortal death.

A need to know the full story drove him to return to work – not for any slave-driver and certainly not for his master, Tefnahkt the Red, but for himself. A soft portion of the wall tempted him with potential secrets underneath, so he resumed his digging there. After the day's work and several more hours into the night, Djedar had created a hole so deep he could nearly stand in it.

Unfortunately, that left him vulnerable. He couldn't see the entrance anymore. Experience told him never to have his back to the door, even in the best of circumstances, but he had no choice. Exchanging his pick for a shovel and putting his lantern at the edge of the pit, he descended into the hole under the wall once more to shovel into the deep, hard earth.

Eventually, he dug deep enough that he could fit his entire frame into the hole and work almost upright under the stone walls of the chamber. Maybe he could even dig a tunnel out of the dig site itself and escape again. Every moment he worked, however, fear of an ambush bit at the back of his neck.

Movement. Someone entered the room behind and above him. Djedar froze, listening, hearing only one set of feet – which meant it probably wasn't a slave-driver. They were smart enough never to walk alone near him after what he'd done. But it also meant whoever was creeping up on him probably wanted to kill him.

"Djedar Rath," said a voice which dripped hatred. "The one who tried to run like a coward and a weakling and got so many of us killed. Traitors shouldn't dig alone."

"You can't betray that to which you swore no loyalty," Djedar replied, looking up to regard a slave he did not recognize.

The other slave – skinny, as slaves were – crouched over the hole with a sneer on his young, scarred face. "Most of us disagree. By being here, we've sworn loyalty. It's commanded of us, by something *higher* than us. All is Lord Tefnahkt the Red's will – we should be grateful that we serve him."

Djedar nodded thoughtfully. "Yes, I've heard. Most of you enjoy being made into a working dog for a man who pretends to be a god."

Outrage widened the other slave's eyes, huge and white. He snatched up the pick from beside the hole and swung it downward. Djedar had barely enough space to jump back and avoid catching the pointed head of the pick in the top of his skull.

Before the other slave could lift the tool again, Djedar grabbed it, pulling on it so hard it jerked the man off-balance, disarming him in the process as the pick slid from his sweat-slicked hands. Djedar dropped the extra makeshift weapon in the pit, keeping his shovel instead. He then climbed out of the hole and rose to his feet while the other slave scrambled back, gnashing his teeth in anger. Even looking up at the taller Djedar, the slave remained defiant.

"You'll pay for your insolence!" he spat. "They'll reward me when I haul your body out, traitor – surely

Lord Tefnahkt will know you're more trouble than you're worth!"

Djedar didn't say a word. He kept the shovel in his hand but held it down to his side, watching the other slave's every movement. He looked like a man possessed, a true believer in his cause, his stare wild and violent.

Too many slaves here didn't care what they were digging up – they had lost their humanity along with any good hope. Those who'd managed to retain their soul had been forcibly purged from Tefnahkt's flock long ago. Save for the occasional old slaves well past their prime, the ones who remained deeply believed in some divine reward from Lord Tefnahkt the Red when they found whatever he had them searching for. They worshiped their master as a greater being, a god among men, who would uplift even the lowest of slaves with his benevolence.

This man certainly believed it. Djedar didn't.

The other slave charged forward. Djedar swung his shovel, but the other slave caught it, wrestling Djedar back a step – toward the pit he'd dug. Trying to make him lose his footing. Djedar didn't budge, standing his ground—

His opponent tried to drive a knee up into his stomach, but Djedar twisted to one side to escape the blow, relinquishing his grip on the shovel in the process. Before the shorter man brought the shovel back around in a wide swing at Djedar's neck, Djedar lunged forward and backhanded him across the jaw, his hand hard as a brick.

But the slave recovered faster than Djedar expected. The point of the shovel met with his side, not quite hard enough to draw blood with its dull head – but hard enough to send pain into his ribs and force him back a step again. Djedar's lost ground spurred the other slave into a frenzy.

He charged. Djedar saw it coming and, at the last moment, side-stepped. He drove forward once the other slave missed his mark, chopping the side of his hand into the other slave's throat. Choking and coughing, the man dropped the shovel, clutching his windpipe. Djedar took hold of the shovel, pried it free from the other slave's weakened grip, and then used his greater height to bodily throw him right into the hole.

He went down in a heap, sputtering and kicking up sand. As the other slave struggled back to his feet and began to claw at the edge of the pit, Djedar lifted the shovel, his gaze cold. The slave stared up at him in bewilderment, as if he hadn't expected recompense – just before Djedar brought the tool down on the crown of his head.

A man dying was a hideous sight. The other slave went still in an instant, going limp like a ragdoll and falling back into the hole in an ugly heap of underfed limbs. Prying the shovel free of bone, Djedar silently worked to fill in the man's newfound grave.

Burying his crime in his night's work didn't bode well for the review of his progress. This would have the slave-drivers believe he'd been sitting around in a dead-end room doing nothing, but his punishment would be far greater still if they discovered a corpse. His masters knew he'd been working this chamber for a while...

"Slave!" a slave-driver called from the doorway. Djedar faced him with as impassive an expression as he could muster. The slave-driver didn't seem to care either way. He barked without paying him much attention, "Mistress Meresamun summons you!"

Perhaps this would allow him some distance from the corpse. Djedar followed the slave-driver through the low doorway and back out into the desert night. There, all the slaves assembled on their knees, heads down, forming great rows lining the walkways around the dig site. The slave-driver behind Djedar gave him a shove toward the line, but Djedar hesitated, watching the woman who could halt all their work with the utterance of a few words.

Behind her trailed a long, red train from the form-fitting *kalasiris* or sheath dress she wore. It left bare her arms, pale shoulders, and glimpses of her legs to show pristinely smooth, light olive skin. Intricate makeup surrounded her dark eyes that flicked over the faces of the kneeling slaves. Gold jewelry wound its way along her upper arms and bangles hung from her wrists while a large, shimmering pectoral covered her upper chest. Beautiful of features, with long, perfectly straight hair of raven black fixed with a golden crown, one could have mistaken Mistress Meresamun for royalty rather than nobility.

Djedar blinked, then furrowed his brow. He had never seen her before. She wore red, like Tefnahkt...

"Kneel," ordered the slave-driver at Djedar's back. Faces of his fellow slaves, some frightened but most simply angry with his noncompliance, glared up at him.

Djedar didn't immediately comply, earning himself a sudden crack on the back of his skull. A whip bit him, hot blood trickling through his very short, shorn hair. He cringed, vision briefly blurring from the pain, but he knew better than to react. With his brief moment of defiance over, he finally knelt like all the other slaves. Unlike them, however, he didn't bow his head.

The woman reached him, having apparently picked up the pace when she heard the whip. She looked at him briefly before frowning over to the man who'd struck him.

"And what," said Meresamun, "was the purpose of that?"

"He wouldn't kneel," the slave-driver answered.

Meresamun stared at him. "You barely gave him time. These people are not to be harmed for no reason. Am I making myself clear?"

Though Djedar didn't look, he heard the slave-driver's feet shuffle in the sand. "Yes, Mistress. I apologize."

"Your feeble apology won't fix his head, nor the illnesses you've been letting sicken so many. Tefnahkt paid a hefty sum for these slaves, and we've had more than enough die over the years, much less those... *disappearances*. I won't have you abusing his property on some petty power trip."

Meresamun turned her attention to Djedar next, looking into his eyes. Djedar knew better than to meet the gazes of his owners, but sometimes he couldn't help himself. She seemed amused by his defiance, taking a step forward – and then grabbing him by the chin.

It took all Djedar's well-practiced willpower not to react. He remained still while she hummed thoughtfully, gripping him hard and pushing his head to one side, admiring his every feature. Djedar still didn't look away from her.

"He's strong," she said. "Handsome, too. Is this the one that escaped?"

"Yes, Mistress," replied another slave-driver nearby.

Meresamun smiled. "Tell me what happened."

"By my understanding, he was born a slave and was later purchased by Tefnahkt..."

"The short version."

"Oh. Uh – he's been a part of some strange events. Many slaves disappeared in a sandstorm, including women and children, leaving only him and a few others behind... plenty of slave-drivers died, too. Don't know what exactly happened, though. I wasn't there. He himself also escaped into the desert once, alone. Killed a slave-driver who'd been watching over him, killed two slaves who tried to stop him. How he survived with no supplies is beyond anyone, but we found him eventually and brought him back. I don't know how long he was out there. He's hard-working; he's just too smart. And vicious." The man sniffed. "He's dangerous. If it'd been up to me, I would've killed him for what he did. But Lord Tefnahkt ordered us not to."

"He was brought before Tefnahkt?"

"Many times. He's one of the only slaves willing to speak to him, give reports. Most of them lose their nerve and start praying to him instead. Tefnahkt used to have this slave take care of his animals after the palace was built, but we've been short on manpower, so we brought him out to the dig a good while ago."

Meresamun turned Djedar's face the other way – then farther still, looking at the whip mark on the back of his head. Djedar didn't move, though his thinning patience did prompt him to inhale a slow, deep breath. Surely she would get bored at some point.

At length, her grip on his chin turned to gentle cradling instead just before her fingers slid away, along with her attention. Djedar swallowed, trying not to show his relief too obviously.

"Interesting," said Meresamun. "He will join those going to the fortress in the morning, then, and tell Tefnahkt of the work done here. If he's already escaped once, keep him in chains, but don't beat him again unless he actually deserves it. Pointless cruelty costs Lord Tefnahkt time and money."

"Yes, Mistress," the slave-driver replied – but then he asked hesitantly, "Who is to lead this caravan?"

Meresamun gave a dismissive wave. "Tefnahkt wanted to see that man who calls himself... what was it? Something like Blacksword."

Djedar couldn't stop himself, saying suddenly, "Blacksword has never led a caravan to the fortress."

The other slave-driver moved behind him; he heard his whip slither in the sand, preparing for another strike. But Meresamun lifted a hand and stopped him, looking at Djedar where he knelt and fearlessly met her gaze.

"Why is that a concern?" she asked.

"We lost a caravan not two weeks ago," the chatty slave-driver behind her put in. "And we lost another one a few months before that."

Meresamun ignored him. Her only focus was Djedar, waiting for him to respond.

"The fortress," Djedar answered calmly, "is beyond the border of the Blasted Wastes."

She nodded. "I know; I've been there. Magnificent, isn't it? Tefnahkt took me there himself more than once." She smiled, as if this was a friendly conversation – she didn't even seem patronizing. She actually seemed genuine. "If Blacksword doesn't get practice now, he won't ever be able to lead caravans to the fortress. Tefnahkt can't lead every caravan personally. *You* seem to have a lot of experience surviving in the desert, don't you? I'm sure you can offer advice."

Djedar scoffed but didn't answer. As if any slave-driver would listen to advice from a slave, particularly a slave who had killed some of their own. Every man knew each trek could be their last. The Blasted Wastes were no place for any mortal, not even one who knew how to survive the harshest of ordinary deserts.

A dry smile tugged at Djedar's lips. He lifted his head and asked, "And who are *you*, Mistress Mereasmun? I've been a slave of Tefnahkt for years... but I've never seen you. I'd certainly remember if I did."

Meresamun laughed. "Well, you're not likely to see me again, I'm afraid. I came to visit in case Tefnahkt himself was here, but he spends most of his time at the fortress now, and going there would be far too perilous a journey without him by my side to protect me. Crossing the Blasted Wastes, even only a few leagues, with naught but these slave-drivers as guardians is unacceptable."

Djedar intoned a thoughtful hum low in his chest, nodding. "I see... a consort, then. His favorite, I imagine."

She only smiled and moved away. "An impressive mouth on that one," she commented to the slave-driver who had answered her questions earlier. "In more ways than one, too. I like him. Try not to let him die in the cursed desert." As she walked away, still looking over the other slaves as she went, Djedar heard her continue: "I'll return to Waset in the morning— wait. What about this one? Why was he beaten? Stop groveling for just one moment, slave..."

She stepped off the path again to examine another slave. Djedar ceased paying any attention, letting his eyes wander up to the stars instead.

They said the stars were signs from the gods, a promise they would always be there watching over. Stars showed the eternity of the deities of the Black Land. Right now, though, not even the stars nor the sliver of the moon that Djedar so enjoyed brought him any comfort. Death frightened him, even if he would never admit it.

Another caravan dared to enter the reaches of the Blasted Wastes... the arrogance of Tefnahkt the Red knew no bounds. Building a fortress out there was more than arrogant enough, outright insane in fact, but to keep sending caravans through these deserts and losing over half of them felt incredibly wasteful. It was no small wonder Tefnahkt currently possessed so little manpower, relatively speaking. His veritable armies of slaves and soldiers had become a relatively small force. How long would it be before Djedar himself ended up in one of those lost caravans, instead of one of the few that actually made it? Before, he had always had the honor of traveling with Lord Tefnahkt himself, which assured their safety. All but one time...

The more he thought about it, however, the more Djedar found himself looking forward to the journey.

Any chance to leave the dig site and return to the open desert once more might be worth it – even if dying one day in the Wastes wouldn't surprise him, with Tefnahkt carelessly pushing everyone's luck.

Starlight cast a strange glow upon the desert, lighting the bleak sands in so deep a blue that the flowing dunes looked like a painted ocean. Not so with the sprawling activity far below, however, where slaves worked themselves to the bone in the middle of those seemingly endless sands, the torchlit dig site nestled deep within the middle of unlivable desolation.

The slaves toiled night and day uncovering ruins so ancient most never would have believed them to be real. Great blocks of sandstone erupted from nowhere in the dig site, and they had already uncovered several statues of various Kemheti gods, particularly the wolf-headed Anubis, standing watch over the long-buried structure hidden deep beneath the desert.

Most would have assumed the simple passage of time had hidden the structures away: strange Kemheti structures in the red sands of Deshret, a foreign land where the people of Kemhet would not ordinarily bury their own. But the one who watched them from afar knew differently: these ruins had been buried on purpose, hidden from the world, sealed away and inaccessible.

From where he rested flat on his chest, the dwarf Buharum stared down at the faraway dig site, watching the slaves go about to and fro like ants.

He perched his bearded chin atop his folded hands. These Men he watched were not like him. Buharum was what they called a *Bes-ak* – children of the bearded god Bes, shortest of all gods but an important figure in the pantheon of the fertile Black Land, Kemhet. The *Besak-ha*, his people, had lived here for many ages.

Most people called his kind a simpler, perhaps less savory name... a dwarf.

Northerners would have jumped to the conclusion that a desert was no place for a dwarf, but not so for him and his people: he had grown up here all his long life, spanning the lives of many mortal Men, and so had his ancestors. Buharum wasn't ancient, by any means, and even he and his people considered this tomb ancient. He never imagined Men would suddenly want to dig it up. How did they even know about its existence at all?

Having lived so long, few things ever came to truly concern him. This, however, did.

"Brother," said a voice at his back, and Buharum craned his neck to regard the speaker, "Solon wants you."

Kukrum, Buharum's brother by clan but not blood relation, stood just beyond the crest of the dune. Like Buharum, Kukrum was also a dwarf, not a mortal Man.

Also like Buharum, he had ruddy skin and a massive black beard of thick, intricate braids and bronze ornamentation covering his entire chest. His suit of lamellar armor perfectly matched Buharum's own, bronze in hue and light in make. At least, such armor was light for a dwarf. The clan-brothers also wore matching helmets, so they almost looked like twins.

"Very well," said Buharum as he rose from his place in the sand, only halfheartedly dusting himself off before trudging back toward the encampment. His companions sat in a rough circle, though they had no fire around which to gather. Light would draw unwanted attention.

Three Men waited for the pair of dwarves. Kukrum chose to make himself look unimportant by standing off to the side, letting the three humans present turn their full attention to Buharum, who folded his arms over his mighty beard.

Mortal Men and immortal dwarf alike had come together in this little group, all part of something greater: the Medjai, an ancient order sworn to protect the land of Kemhet, guarding its pharaoh and its people... and keeping safe its ancient secrets.

The Medjai, of course, were a much larger organization than this trio of humans and two Besak-ha. But they were the only ones who had been available to undertake this particular mission – and the Medjai as a whole remained unaware just how desperate a situation this had become. Someone actually uncovering the Tomb of Ankhu seemed impossible.

Back to the matter at hand, however, Buharum looked over his other companions. Rarely did Buharum ever see any of the Men of their group lighten up, but right now they looked so grim that he almost wanted to kick sand in their faces. Worrying themselves to death would hardly help the situation, and their lifespans were short enough already.

Their leader rose to his feet. Solon Sun-Eyes was an Imperial born in Kemhet and wholly integrated into their ways, as good as a Kemheti himself. He wore only simple white clothing, a composite bow and quiver on his back, and a knife at his side. His revealing attire showed off his skin – bronzed, yet still fairer than many Kemhetis – as well as his heavy muscles and his sizable gut from too much beer. He kept his body and face shaved perfectly slick, save for his dark eyebrows. This only served to highlight his bright hazel eyes, as well as his still more unusual markings.

Black, jagged tattoos covered his body in strange, disturbing, winding patterns. They touched all his limbs, his neck, and even his head and face. Runes written in the same black ink nestled between the assorted curves and prongs of the sundry designs.

Even Buharum had no idea what any of it meant, including the runic letters. Supposedly, the Dwarves had long ago mastered the art of ancient runic magic, said to be the language of the creator gods themselves.

However, Buharum had never actually bothered studying it, himself. Far too complicated – and probably a drag.

"Buharum," said the incredibly tattooed Solon in his voice like thunder and grinding stone, "what did you see?"

"Plenty of movement, even now," Buharum replied. "They're always active. I can't see their faces from here, but I'd bet they're as exhausted as you lot look."

"This is no joking matter."

Buharum shrugged. "Oh, I know it's not. Of everything we protect, this is the most important. But..."

"But nothing," cut in the only woman present, a knife-wielder by the name of Farrah, clad in robes of deep crimson. She hailed from the vast and sprawling Deshret, the Red Land, where they currently were. She flipped her long, black hair away from her swarthy face, eyes gleaming with hatred. "I watched the camp earlier. There are guards, but we've faced forces their size before. We could split them up and pick them off – then we go into the camp and take out the slaves."

Solon glared at her. "No. We do *not* harm slaves under any circumstances."

Farrah scoffed. "Even if those slaves are helping to end the world?"

"Here now, they haven't even found the blasted door yet, and the world's not gonna *end*. You're just catastrophizing early," Buharum remarked. Everyone ignored him – lost in their own arguments, as usual. Leave it to them to not listen to a dwarf.

"Yes," Solon snapped back at her.

Farrah threw her hands in the air. "Fine."

"It wasn't by their doing that they serve those with evil in their hearts," Solon went on like some kind of poet, straightening the quiver on his back.

Next, the tallest and darkest figure among them spoke: the third human in the group, one who called himself Dunewalker. "Inspiring words," he said, "but *all* Men carry evil in their hearts."

Everyone fell silent, at least for a moment. Dunewalker was the eldest of the mortals present, a few years older than Solon, leaving Farrah the youngest of all. Buharum wasn't sure of his exact age, but if Dunewalker didn't keep his head and his face perfectly shaven like Solon, Buharum guessed he would've had a decent touch of grey in his hair.

Dunewalker was an impressive man, particularly given his lean musculature left largely visible in his simple outfit of a leather harness, a vest, and a metal plate strapped over his heart, along with trousers and boots. Like Solon, he wore a composite bow and quiver, as well. Dunewalker's skin was darker than anyone else present, a rich ebony in hue. He was an Axan. As deeply south as they were now, so far from Kemhet and the borders of the Achaean Empire, his people were not an uncommon sight. Dunewalker's people had little desire to travel so far as to mingle with the folk of other lands, and Dunewalker himself seemed to feel the same way, especially since he never shared his real name.

Everyone looked grimmer than ever, their thoughts turning inward.

Buharum rolled his eyes. "Is it a quality of not living very long that makes you all so damn serious?"

Dunewalker flashed him a quick, bright grin, though Buharum didn't read mirth in it. "I've never met a Besak who loves to flaunt his immortality as you do, Buharum. What made you *that* way?"

"We are all immortal, Dune," Solon put in. "The Besak-ha aren't taken by age, but our souls will continue their journeys when we leave these bodies behind."

"Great," Farrah muttered, "another sermon..."

But Dunewalker straightened up and said, "He's right. And that's what concerns me most – the creature and its immortal soul still trapped in that... labyrinthian tomb."

For the first time since the conversation started, Buharum's fellow dwarf Kukrum spoke up from the edge of their sad little camp. "Do you think those poor slaves even know what they're digging up?"

"Would it matter if they did?" Farrah remarked. "They're slaves. They have to do what they're told."

Solon went to his horse and removed a bedroll from the saddle. He returned to their sitting circle to toss the blanket to the ground, pointedly spreading it over the sand.

"Get comfortable," he ordered. "We'll take turns watching the dig site. You're right, Farrah: slaves must do as they are told. That's why we're going to wait until a convoy leaves, bound for their master. Then, we follow that back to whoever is behind uncovering the tomb, and we put an end to this."

An 'end' to what, exactly? Buharum wanted to ask as he sat down to clean his crescent axe, just for something to do. But he didn't bother voicing his question. Why anyone would want to dig up the tomb of Ankhu seemed unfathomable. The only thing in that place was death.

Death – and one of the greatest evils the world had ever known.

Sleep was all but impossible to find in a slave camp. Somehow, though, Djedar managed enough rest to awaken alert and ready to face his fate. He went with silent reservation, herded alongside a handful of other slaves across the eternally bustling dig site.

Day had not yet broken as they prepared to leave. Torches and lanterns still chased away the shadows throughout the dig, and exhausted slaves toiled with glazed-over eyes everywhere Djedar turned, the whips of their drivers and blind loyalty to their master keeping them working. A thin veil of early morning light, pale against the dismal deep blue sky, had only just begun to chase away the stars. It crept into the far edges of the horizon and offered hope of respite to the night-working slaves.

The walk was long, given the size of the dig. When they at last reached the convoy, Djedar didn't find it impressive. Five horses were assembled, each intended for a slave-driver. One enclosed wooden wagon stood at the ready, two horses pulling it; the wagon was shaped almost like a small ship, not unlike some Kemheti funerary barge, which immediately put Djedar ill at ease. But it seemed at home in the sands, given its broad wheels and design suitable for desert travel.

There was also a camel loaded down with supplies and tied to the hind of the wagon by a single rope. Camels were a rare sight in Djedar's birth land, as the people of Kemhet considered them unclean and unfit for use even as a pack animal, preferring donkeys or oxen. Here in Deshret, however, camels were used for all sorts of purposes, even as mounts.

The slave-driver who called himself Blacksword hadn't yet mounted his horse, marching around barking orders while spittle flew from his thick, black beard. Long, curly hair of the same color hung past his shoulders, and dark, beady eyes set under a heavy brow made him look meaner than a serpent. His deeply ruddy skin told of his Deshreti birth and heritage of desert wanderers, as did his attire of robes to protect from the sun and several belts holding blades.

"Kemheti!" Blacksword barked, wheeling to glare at Djedar. "I was told you've traveled this way before."

"Yes," Djedar answered.

"I was also told you've survived in the desert alone for days."

"I have."

"And no one knows how you did it."

This time, Djedar didn't bother responding.

Blacksword continued anyway, undeterred. "I come from a tribe not far from here. My family has walked the Red Lands since long before you and whatever slave spawned you were even lifting bricks. I do *not* want your advice unless I explicitly ask for it, is that understood?"

Djedar replied with a smile, "I'll remember that."

Blacksword spat a thick wad of saliva in the sand at Djedar's feet. Had he asked, Djedar would've advised him promptly that wasting his water in such a way wouldn't get him far, no matter how long his ancestors had lived here. As it was, he didn't say a word.

"Good," Blacksword snapped, turning away. "Put him in chains, as Meresamun ordered!"

Two more slave-drivers came forward, heavy chains rattling in their hands. One knelt to shackle Djedar's ankles, while the other tightened irons around his wrists, connecting those to a metal ring enclosed about his neck. Djedar, like all the other slaves, wore nothing more than a *shendyt*, or essentially a civilized Kemheti loincloth, and the many chains bit into his bare skin.

Such elaborate restraints drew the eyes of his peers, the slaves watching from the wagon. From the looks on the faces of one or two, they knew why he wore such shackles.

But Djedar merely flashed a quick smile to the men who had put him in chains and said, "Impressive. Quite the fashion statement for seeing Tefnahkt."

"*Lord* Tefnahkt," one slave corrected harshly.

"You'll walk *alongside* the wagon for now," Blacksword said, motioning Djedar forward with a swing of his arm. To another slave-driver, he said, "Tie a rope so he can't wander off."

When a rope had been fastened around his chains, the other end tied to the side of the wagon, Blacksword was finally satisfied. Djedar didn't comment all the while, already at work figuring out how he could escape his bonds if the need arose.

They set off in silence, save for the creaking wagon and shifting sand around the horses' hooves. No road stretched before them for their travel as they started in a seemingly random direction away from the dig site, into the vastness of the desert. The sand beneath them had been marked only lightly, subtle but noticeable, telling of other caravans that had come this way before – others belonging to Tefnahkt, over half of which had been lost in the desolation of the Wastes.

Hopefully they wouldn't meet the same fate.

Resigned, Djedar walked alongside the wagon, chains rattling with every step. At least they hadn't put a muzzle on him, though it almost surprised him, given Blacksword's attitude. The shackles on his wrists cut into him almost as badly as the ones on his ankles, so he turned his attention outward.

Emptiness surrounded them, a sea of seemingly endless sand in all directions. Soon the dig site disappeared over the rolling dunes that still carried a faintly blue hue, so early was the morning light. The convoy moved between the dunes at a slow but steady pace. As they traveled, the sun came all too soon and lent its golden light to the desert, turning the sky a brilliant blue.

Civilization was a foreign concept to these timeless red deserts of deep Deshret, so far from anything that even the wandering tribes of the Deshreti people dared not set foot here. These lands rested on the doorstep of the Blasted Wastes, a place no mortal man should tread after its accursed fate.

Djedar, however, didn't know many details of its fate. He knew little of history and culture, though he learned whatever he could when he got the chance. Still, most everyone in the Southron lands knew at least some of the tales... though apparently there were those who still hadn't heard them.

Several hours into their trek, around the time Djedar's legs began to ache from shuffling in chains beside a horse-drawn wagon traveling treacherous sands, one of the slaves riding on a seat jutting from the wagon's side gave him a long look and said, "Are you the man who almost escaped?"

Djedar feigned ignorance, regarding the other slave with a look of wonder. "Someone almost escaped?"

The slave stared at him briefly. "They say he killed several men."

"Well, I hope we don't meet him. He sounds dangerous."

"They say he wandered the desert, and no one knows how he survived. No one goes out in those dunes and lives."

Djedar shrugged, manacles clinking loudly. "We're in those dunes right now. Are you expecting to die?"

"What? No. We have supplies and—" He paused and stared again, then blurted, "Are you simple?"

"Relatively. I'm only a slave, after all." Djedar side-eyed his would-be interrogator, the faintest hint of a smile playing on his lips. "What about you?"

He scoffed. "Tell me about the Wastes, if you're so smart."

"You've never made this journey before, then?"

Suddenly the other slave balked, shrinking like someone had raised a whip. "No. Is it true there are monsters that don't feel the bite of steel?"

Djedar almost considered actually telling him what he knew: great mage wars long ago had corrupted the region with so much magic that it seeped into the very spirits of the land, changing them forever – everything from the sands themselves to the wildlife had become abominations, immune to most mortal weaponry. The Wastes were a place where directions made no sense and living nightmares hunted in the night, longing for the sweet taste of human flesh over all else.

But he said instead, testing the waters, "Don't you trust the power of Tefnahkt to protect you?"

The slave perked up in an instant, puffing his chest out and answering, "That's true – you're right. Lord Tefnahkt commands these lands. He'll watch over us, won't he? He watches over all who serve him, even the lowest slaves."

Djedar snorted. "*I* never said he'd watch over us."

The slave stared at him for speaking blasphemy. "Then you don't believe?"

Well, that concluded the conversation. Djedar let his gaze wander over the horizon, watching the waves of heat shimmering in the air and focusing on putting one foot before the other.

The slave added after a moment, sounding angry, "You *should* believe. He'll see us safely to the fortress – it is his bidding."

Djedar said nothing. The dig site and beyond were in Set's lands, the red deserts away from Kemhet's borders, but not even Set's merciless reach extended into the Wastes. What dark god exerted its bidding over the place they were going, Djedar didn't know, but he knew for certain it wasn't Lord Tefnahkt the Red.

Shame the slave who spoke to him was yet another zealot. In a way, he wouldn't have minded a conversation. Something to take his mind off his suffering, the way his feet ached and his legs burned, his throat pleading for a drink.

Then he almost collapsed.

But he didn't. Djedar only stumbled, his assortment of chains trying to deafen him once again with their incessant clinking. He righted himself quickly, straightening up and dismissing his pained grimace to replace it with a grim stare instead.

Blacksword slowed his steed, throwing Djedar a look. He was the only slave who'd been forced to walk, so he stood out, with or without restraints.

Another slave-driver looked also, then shot Blacksword a confused glare. "You let him waste away, and our heads will roll for it. Lord Tefnahkt won't hesitate to punish all of us if we let his animal-keeper die. *I'm* not feeding that damn elephant or anything else in his menagerie."

"Then maybe he should be keeping the animals instead of digging," Blacksword answered, taking a long pull from an animal skin doubtlessly full of *heqet*: essentially, nutritious beer.

"You know Lord Tefnahkt wants the slaves helping with the dig."

Another moment of silence passed. Hooves beat gently in the sands, the wheels creaking on rhythmically. Djedar thought about letting himself fall just to see what they would do, but pride kept his legs moving and his head high.

"Blacksword," the other slave-driver hissed again, insistently.

"I won't die just because you don't like this stupid slave," a third slave-driver snapped. "Lord Tefnahkt favors that one. Whether you see his reasons or not, it is his will that the slave lives."

Rolling his eyes, Blacksword finally gave another wave of his hand and ordered, "Put him on the wagon – and give him something to drink. We don't need him slowing us down."

The convoy's pace slackened long enough for the other slaves to help Djedar. No one had lifted a finger to assist him all the while, but now the slaves hurried to grab his arms and haul him up onto an exterior seat; apparently he still didn't warrant a resting place inside the wagon itself. One man then passed a skin of *heqet*, which Djedar took and uncorked without a word, forgetting his long-fought-for dignity and drinking deeply.

The deeper they went into the desert, the more Djedar lost track of time, as was wont to happen when one neared the dark magic of the Wastes. Time didn't matter, anyway: all that mattered was staying alive. The struggle for survival took his remaining focus, as Blacksword occasionally ordered him down from his seat, forcing him to walk himself numb before his fellow slave-drivers reminded him that Lord Tefnahkt wanted Djedar alive and capable of speech.

Eventually, Blacksword lost interest in him, which told Djedar they were nearing the Wastes. The looks of resolve and general annoyance on the slave-drivers' faces steadily melted into fear and concern – all except Blacksword, who remained confident. Djedar couldn't decide if that worried him more or less.

Then, things changed. The land around them became something different. Slowly at first, Djedar picked up on even the subtlest hint that they were entering the Blasted Wastes. It started with a strange sensation in the air, almost like humidity: not something a desert often felt. A sticky, cloying sensation settled onto his skin thicker than the sweat already coating him.

"Djedar Rath," Blacksword called, catching his attention. "Is that your name, slave?"

"Yes," Djedar answered wearily. "What?"

"Consider this me asking for whatever wisdom you're supposed to have. Are we going the right way?"

Djedar allowed a pause before answering, "You don't know which way you're going?"

"*I'm* navigating," snapped another slave-driver. "I'll take care of it, Blacksword. We're going the right way."

Blacksword didn't say another word, looking away from Djedar; that meant he wasn't supposed to speak. Djedar fell silent once again, slipping back into thought.

Next, the sands began to change. The red sand steadily deepened and grew pale, becoming very faintly grey. Then, every grain around them suddenly looked ashen, until all the various bright blues, greens, reds, and whites worn by the convoy stood out in an almost frightening way, like they entered a world where color did not belong.

As if the utter desolation of the unforgiving red deserts in Deshret hadn't been terrible enough, the Blasted Wastes made any man long for the comfort of at least the familiar, no matter how arid and dangerous. Because, for every peril in an ordinary wasteland, the realm that had once been the Empire of Sinkarya so long ago held ten perils more... and none of them familiar.

Worse still, perhaps, was the fog. The longer they traveled, the heavier it became. As day fell into night, clouds settled around them, just as colorless as the sand under their feet. The other slaves wore masks of terror, while every slave-driver's hands rested on his weapons. Djedar steepled his fingers together before him and stared off into the distance, brow knit, silent as the grave.

"Is night falling?" asked one slave, keeping his voice low, as if disturbing the stillness might kill him. "I can't tell."

"Shouldn't we be resting by now?" said another. "I feel like I could fall off the cart."

"Blacksword," a slave-driver called from horseback, "let's make camp before we go even deeper into this accursed place."

Blacksword roughly pulled his steed to a halt, wheeling to face the convoy he led. "Make camp!" he shouted. "Tomorrow, we ride day and night! See that the animals are fed first and keep the slaves together!"

The wagon halted on a flat patch of sand away from any dunes, the slave-drivers dismounting and motioning the slaves off their seats to help set up camp. Djedar leapt down and watched everyone hurry around him, bringing out supplies for the horses first, while others set up a perimeter.

No one paid him any heed; he couldn't help, shackled as he was. Djedar wandered to the back of the wagon and looked at the camel standing there chewing gods-knew-what, as they hadn't passed even a thorny shrub for days. Djedar lifted a hand, and the camel lowered its nose into Djedar's touch.

"You wouldn't get far on that beast," remarked a nearby slave, "if that's what you were hoping, traitor."

Djedar gave a low chuckle, but he didn't answer.

Everything seemed reasonably alright until Blacksword gave another shout— "Asan, get over here!" The slave beside Djedar immediately went to answer the call, but Blacksword kept issuing orders. "All of you, set up torches around the camp! Keep them lit all night, I don't want a single one going out!"

Those words sent Djedar's stomach dropping so low that his gnawing hunger, which bordered on starvation, was instantly forgotten. Blacksword patrolled around the camp on foot, one hand gripping the hilt of his namesake black *khopesh* sword sheathed at his hip: a wicked crescent-shaped and axe-like blade, curved but still bearing a vicious point at the end despite its relatively squared-off tip. Djedar gave Blacksword such a deep stare that it drew his attention.

"What?" prompted the head slave-driver.

"Ask me for my advice," said Djedar, despite the way Blacksword glared at him indignantly.

"Fine, if you have to be cute about it. Tell me."

"Torches aren't a good idea."

Blacksword laughed, his yellowed teeth colorful against the grey world. "Fire drives away animals, Rath."

"These aren't animals. The creatures that live here *understand* fire; they don't fear it. If you set up torches, you're good as inviting them to a banquet."

Yet again Blacksword waved his hand. "Go to sleep, slave."

With that, he turned away and resumed barking orders. Djedar scoffed, setting his jaw, but he said no more. He retrieved his bedroll and threw it underneath the body of the wagon, spreading it out with difficulty thanks to the chains still squeezing his wrists.

"What are you doing?" asked the same slave who'd spoken to him during the journey, the one who thought Tefnahkt would keep them safe. "You really *are* simple, aren't you?"

"*Simply* trying to stay alive," Djedar replied, flashing the slave a brief smile.

"You're like a child hiding under his bed."

"Under the bed is where the monsters live. Your mother didn't tell you that?"

The slave laughed. "That makes even less sense. Why would you hide under there, then?"

"Because in the Wastes, the monsters *don't* hide, so under the bed is vacant – and I'll be taking it." Djedar lifted one shackled hand, kissed where his thumb rested against the middle of his forefinger, and used that to motion a smooth gesture like a salute off his forehead. "Good night."

The bewildered slave watched Djedar crunch himself to squeeze between the wagon wheels and then underneath the length of the cart's body, stretching out so he wouldn't get run over if it moved. Bending down, the slave insisted upon staring at him some more. Djedar quirked a long, dark eyebrow and stared right back.

"No, I'm not sharing, if that's what you're going to ask."

"You're insane," declared the slave.

Djedar frowned. "I thought I was simple."

The man shook his head and moved off. Thanking the gods for his relative solace, Djedar at last attempted to get some rest.

Not long after he drifted into a faint and unrestful slumber, still plagued by thoughts, a sound pulled him from his poor attempt at sleep.

He opened his eyes to an even darker desert night, fog masking the moon and stars from view. Only a faint spill of pallid glow, distilled by the strange mist, lit the grey sands. The light of the torches around the halted convoy still burned, casting an orange haze by which one could see hints of the nothingness around them.

A whisper drifted over the camp. Djedar knit his brow and sat up as far as he could without hitting his head on the underbelly of the wagon, looking around. Everyone else still slept, various slaves and slave-drivers snoozing on their bedrolls, scattered around in the ring of torches. A few seemed uneasy, shifting now and then, perhaps partially awake – but clearly not awake enough to hear...

"*Djedar*," an otherworldly voice called. It sounded almost like Blacksword, and yet the more he thought about it, the more he knew it wasn't the lead slave-driver. This voice breathed his name half through its nose and half in its throat, ending it in a hiss that sent a chill up Djedar's spine. Cautiously, Djedar dragged himself out from under the wagon, sand partially masking the sound of his assorted chains.

Nothing moved. There were still no signs of life around them. A quick gust of wind stirred the ashen sand, sending air too cold even for a desert night billowing over the camp and disturbing the many blankets and bedrolls. The horses woke, shifting on their hooves, and the torchlight danced ominously.

Then two torches went out.

It made Djedar start, whirling to face the sudden darkness. But nothing moved there either. At least, not anything he saw.

"*Djedar, come to me,*" the voice whispered again like someone stood right over his shoulder. His skin prickled along his neck, and he turned again to face the sound – only to see that two more torches had gone out.

They were being hunted.

"Horus have mercy," Djedar muttered under his breath.

Finally, a few others in the caravan started to stir. Another slave nearby sat up, blinking in alarm.

Then came the voice again. *"Asan,"* it called. The slave beside Djedar reacted instantly, looking in the direction of the voice that sounded so like and yet unlike their leader, Blacksword.

Without a word, the slave Asan got to his feet and began marching right toward it – away from the remaining ring of torches. Djedar didn't move, but he snapped, "What're you doing?"

"Blacksword calls," replied Asan. "You may not care about your duties to Lord Tefnahkt, but I do. Blacksword serves his will."

And he resumed walking. Against his better judgment, Djedar blurted, "Go out there and you'll walk right down a monster's throat."

"Monsters can't *speak*," Asan scoffed, but regardless, Djedar's words made him hesitate...

At least until the voice called again, sounding so much like Blacksword that even Djedar almost wondered. *"Asan – come. Now!"* it beckoned.

And so the slave went. No longer hesitating, he strode right out into the fog. Djedar almost had to admire how the depths of Asan's stupidity lent him such bravery—

He heard a distant crunch. No scream broke the stillness at any point, but Djedar knew the muffled meaty crack of a human neck. Such a sound was unmistakable.

Then something laughed.

It wasn't a human laugh. It wasn't the cold chuckle of an assassin, nor the triumphant laugh of a warrior. It was a distorted noise, throaty and undulating, first high almost like a hyena and then so low it resembled the deep baying of a hound, and yet not familiar like either. Djedar didn't have to see its source to know such a voice was not of the natural world.

His blood ran cold, and for a moment, he couldn't make his own muscles move.

More slaves awoke, and something thudded within the wagon. Blacksword came staggering out, still wearing all his gear. He looked around with wild eyes before his gaze settled hard on Djedar, but only briefly. Another slave-driver woke up nearby, and Blacksword turned to him instead.

"Who said that?" he asked.

"I didn't hear anything," replied the other slave-driver.

Djedar took the general confusion as a chance to search the camp. One slave-driver had a long, straight-bladed knife in a dark sheath near his pillow. Djedar scooped it up, tucking it less than comfortably behind the front of his belt. If Blacksword saw a knife on him, he wouldn't have it long.

"Blacksword?" called one of the slaves, catching Djedar's attention again. He started off into the desert like the first man, disappearing into the mist.

"No, you idiot – I'm here!" Blacksword bellowed after him. "Get *back* here!"

Too late. Up went a scream this time, piercing the night – the wrenching cry of a man's final shout before his death. Next came the meaty crunch, this one louder than the first.

"Fools! Stay in the camp!" Blacksword ordered, drawing his blade. "Stay close to the wagon – no one is ordering you out into the desert!"

But Djedar hesitated. He watched the slave-drivers usher the remaining slaves back around the wagon. The horses snorted and stamped at the sand, ears flat against their heads. If he ever *were* to escape, this would be a perfect chance. But to escape out into the Wastes...

"*Djedar,*" the voice whispered practically in his ear. He cringed and hurried back to the convoy, though the shackles around his ankles slowed him down. No – he couldn't escape. Not right now, not while they were being hunted—

Something lunged from the mist.

A massive paw like a lion's appeared only long enough to knock a retreating slave off his feet – and then something grabbed him, too quickly to be seen, and dragged him screaming into the night.

Two slaves remained, other than Djedar, and both of them tried to climb up into the wagon to hide. The slave-drivers shoved them away, though one pushed an axe into a slave's hand. Blacksword stood his ground despite the obvious fear on his face, sweat rolling down his brow and cheeks, making his thick beard glisten in the flickering torchlight that grew ever weaker.

Djedar did a quick head-count – three other slave-drivers were missing. Only four remained, including Blacksword. When had the monster picked them off?

Silence fell so suddenly no one knew what to do with it. They just stood, weapons drawn – save for Djedar, who remained in chains, keeping near the wagon and ready to duck underneath it at any moment.

No one spoke. No one moved. Only the terrified snorting and occasional whinny of the horses, along with the labored breathing of the terrified convoy, broke the utter stillness.

Until, finally, Blacksword barked an order. "Release three of the horses."

"But—" started another slave-driver, but Blacksword cut him off.

"Do it!"

Another man cut the three of the horses' leads tethering them to the wagon, and off the trio of steeds went, charging into the night and disappearing. The sound of their hooves faded quickly into nothing once more.

"The beast will chase them," Blacksword said confidently, straightening up again. "Gather the torches and put everything back in the wagon. We're leaving."

Another slave-driver coughed out a terrified laugh, even as one of the remaining slaves quickly moved to do as ordered. "To hell with the *torches*, let's get out of here!"

Djedar scanned the area once again while the survivors quickly gathered their things to leave. The slave who went to retrieve the torches did not return, and another of those torches had gone out. So little light remained that Djedar didn't take a single step away from the wagon. The mist around them drew ever nearer, closing in, further diffusing the already meager moonlight into a fuzzy, dim haze.

He could barely see a thing.

And then a shape, enormous and dark, leapt from the mist and straight into what remained of the camp.

It lunged, haunches thicker and more powerful even than a lion, its massive jaws open wide. The remaining torchlight let Djedar glimpse a tawny hide with faint ruddy stripes like a predator – and mismatched hind legs, black with cloven hooves like a beast of burden.

It was one of the distorted abominations of the Wastes, a single creature composed of many things twisted together.

The monster was so great and its jaws so vast it snatched a slave-driver up whole. It bared a long row of stark white teeth as it bit down, crushing the screaming man's spine to stop his struggling before downing his still-twitching corpse in a single swallow, so powerful that the sound of it reverberated off the sides of the wagon like the toll of a death knell.

It tore into the remaining slave-drivers. And while his men and the slaves were slaughtered in the mist only a few feet away, Blacksword backed right into Djedar. He turned to stare at him, a changed man, as if driven mad on the spot – but Djedar hadn't changed a bit.

"Unlock me," Djedar ordered, locking gazes with him. Blacksword's dark eyes stared at him, full of wild fear. "Let me fight or we'll *both* die—"

Blacksword sputtered, "I – I won't—"

The laughing sounded again, twisted and wrong. Still the sounds of battle rang, screams of fear and anguish. Blacksword froze, somehow going even paler. Djedar twisted the chains around his wrists, gnashing his own white teeth like the beast devouring them all.

"Ammit eat your coward heart, I said *unlock me!*" Djedar snarled. No longer protesting, Blacksword fumbled into a pocket on his robe and threw something in Djedar's direction. A small ring of iron keys landed in the grey sand nearby.

"Unlock *yourself*, slave," Blacksword snapped, lifting his blade again with newfound fury. "I'll have this beast dead by the time you're finished!"

Djedar dived for the keys without hesitation, fumbling past several in the ring and trying each as quickly as he could— finally, one worked. The manacles around his wrist came off with a creak, and he pried his hands free, wrestling with the chain still dangling from his neck...

Blacksword screamed. Djedar ducked instinctively as he saw, in the corner of his eye, something flying right at him.

Blacksword's corpse.

The head slave-driver's body thudded into the side of the sturdy wagon so hard it almost toppled over sideways. Blacksword's lifeless form landed face-first in the sand, unmoving, black blade still clenched in one hand. The remaining horses whinnied and screamed, rearing, pulling and chewing desperately at their tethers while the pack camel bellowed to the heavens.

Djedar dropped low and rolled to one side, once again taking shelter under the wagon. Quietly, he shifted onto his back to reach for the dagger he'd concealed—

But he froze. He wasn't alone.

First came a set of paws bearing long black talons, stalking toward the wagon so soundlessly one never would have imagined the size of the monster bearing them. A set of black hooves like a bull's followed after them. Both were painted by spatters of fresh blood.

It moved closer, scarcely making a sound. A rope snapped – a horse had pulled free of its lead.

The steed ran off into the night, as the others had done before, but the monster paid it no mind. It was interested in man-flesh, not that of beasts. Such a meal was surely a rare delicacy in the Wastes, a place every human had long since learned to avoid – everyone except Tefnahkt and his men, the fools who wouldn't listen to a common slave.

Djedar silently cursed his fate. He remained still, almost flat on his back and wishing he'd never repositioned himself to reach for the pathetic dagger. No wound marred the monster's hide that he could see, as if the weapons of every man in the convoy had glanced right off it. As if it merely shrugged off the conventional weapons of mortals – like the stories said... except for one scratch.

He paused. 'Blacksword.' His black blade...

The monster stopped. It stood perfectly still. Djedar didn't even breathe – but it didn't matter. It struck.

Claws snatched for him, one massive set of talons reaching under the wagon and catching on his upper leg, hooking his flesh – and starting to drag him backward. Djedar gritted his teeth, hands shooting up to grab hold of the wagon's underside and anchor himself. The beast pulled harder, almost taking his leg off – but Djedar wrenched himself free of its claws, opening a wound in his leg that sprayed blood.

Somehow he swallowed a cry as he rolled over again and dragged himself forward on his elbows, crawling over the thick sand—

The shelter over his head disappeared.

In a single swipe, the abomination knocked the entire wagon aside, revealing its helpless prey underneath. Horses and the camel still tied to the wagon went flying and shrieking. Djedar didn't even have enough time to turn his head and look up at the beast before he felt it on his back.

Weight pushed onto him, claws set into his skin again – and they ripped, crushing and tearing. It rent his back open so deeply the pain reached the very bones of his spine. Agony blinded him. Hot blood covered everything below his shoulders. Djedar screamed.

But he reached out for the black-bladed sword still beside Blacksword's corpse, fingers closing around its hilt—

Just as he turned. Just as the monster's gaping jaws descended upon him – and all he knew was darkness.

Death. From where they had made camp, the small group of Medjai heard something in the distance over two rolling grey dunes.

Screams drifted on the wind and made the dwarf Buharum sit bolt upright, his blood turning to ice. Their massive and seemingly always shirtless leader, Solon, stomped into the middle of camp and swept up his bedroll in one quick snatch, rolling it expertly and stuffing it onto the saddle of his horse.

"If everyone in the convoy is killed, we'll *never* find that fortress," he said, swinging himself up onto his steed. "Get up – we have to help them!"

Everyone leapt into action. Their simple camp, with no fires burning at all, was packed within seconds. Horses were mounted and set off at a canter over the sands, the lot of them wide awake and riding hard.

Suddenly, silence fell.

The screaming ceased. Sounds of battle faded into the stark nothing of the Wastes once more. Solon slowed his horse and lifted a hand, wordlessly ordering everyone to do the same. Buharum did as he was told, his clan-brother Kukrum clinging to his middle as they rode double, but he still urged his horse closer to Solon's to see why he'd stopped.

A corpse lay crumpled before them, twisted unnaturally with his head on askew and a portion of his broken spine silhouetted through his skin. The body looked like an afterthought, something thrown aside from a greater confrontation.

Solon stayed only a moment before his horse sidestepped the destroyed corpse that had once been a slave. Buharum spied another contorted body that also seemed tossed in a fit of rage, no doubt by something unimaginably strong. No tracks or signs of disturbance in the sands around it told how the body came there, so it could have only been thrown – but from where?

As much as something in him wanted to comment, Buharum bit his tongue. Next, they found the body of a horse. Then three horses and a camel, barely a few feet away from a strange shape jutting from a grey dune...

It was an entire wagon, shattered and broken, half on its side and half on its top.

The stench of blood reached him, turning his stomach. Buharum had fought many times in his life longer than a mortal human's, yet the smell always riled some nausea in him.

At last, they came upon a circle of what looked like torches that had gone out. What fools burned fires in the Blasted Wastes?

In the middle of the circle lay a massive abomination, twisted in death throes. Chimeran, the Imperials called them – an accursed beast spawned from magical corruption. In the darkness and fog, Buharum couldn't make out how many different animal features it had, though he did see black hooves, massive paws with curved talons almost like an eagle's, and a tawny hide.

The tip of something sharp and black jutted up from its distorted head that wasn't quite a hyena or a lion. Something had pierced its skull from underneath.

Buharum walked his horse around to the monster's front, staring at its jaws enormous enough to swallow a grown man whole. In those jaws he saw a hint of deep olive skin – a man's arm. The rest of him was half pinned beneath the monster's glutted bulk, as somehow his arm had remained attached to his body.

Solon wasted no time. He dismounted and strode up to the dead monster before looking back at the others and saying, "We need to get this off him."

"You don't really think he's still alive?" Buharum asked as he and Kukrum took turns climbing down the short rope ladder that let them clamber up onto their high horse's saddle.

"There's a lot of blood, Solon," Farrah added. "I'm pretty sure a lot of it is his."

"He looks like a slave," Dunewalker pointed out grimly.

It was true: the man underneath the monster wore no shirt on his back. Then again, neither did Solon, though he did so by choice.

"Get on each side," Solon ordered, ignoring the remarks. "Farrah, Kukrum, you're with me. Dunewalker, help Buharum."

The Medjai split up and went to either side of the abomination, lifting it on the count of three. Even their combined strength had trouble moving it, but they hauled it far enough away to uncover the slave's body.

The sight made Buharum cringe. The slave lay twisted, clad only in a simple *shendyt* loincloth, his blood soaking the ashen sands around him until they looked almost black. His eyes were shut and his body unmoving...

No – it wasn't. He breathed. Drawing closer, Buharum saw the slave's chest rising and falling weakly.

"He... killed it," Dunewalker said, voice low with amazement. Buharum turned just in time to see him reach into the beast's maw and grip something, yanking hard until he removed a bloodied, black sword from the beast's head. "He ran this through its skull. The blade is void iron."

Kukrum's eyebrows shot up so far they almost displaced his helmet. "He must've struck faster than a serpent."

"How did a slave get a void iron blade?" Farrah wondered aloud. "I'd say the dwarves charge an arm and a leg for it, but that still wouldn't be enough payment."

Buharum scoffed, though he couldn't deny the way in which the dwarves protected the magical metals they mined from deep within the bowels of the world. Void iron was a truly rare material mined from a place called Nidavellir, the cavernous realm that existed below the surface world of mortals. Only Buharum's fair-skinned kinfolk, the dwarves of the mountains, mined and forged it. Void iron was so black it ate light rather than reflecting it, and tales told of how the metal was composed of the void left from before the gods had crafted the realms: a void so powerful that the metal could absorb all forms of magic. Nothing else was capable of such a feat.

"I doubt it was his," Dunewalker said to Farrah.

"This fellow's not going to last long," said Kukrum, who knelt alongside the slave, looking him over. "His leg's been torn open and he's lost a lot of blood."

"But he's still alive for now. Let's move him," Solon commanded. "Gently. Dunewalker!"

Dunewalker came over without a word as they lifted the slave, revealing still more blood underneath him. They carried him to a bedroll Farrah had spread out in preparation. But before they lowered him onto it, Dunewalker held up a hand.

"Turn him over," he said.

So they did – and Buharum, with his self-proclaimed cast iron stomach, almost lost his last meal.

The man was lucky his spine was still intact. How anyone could survive wounds like those for longer than a few minutes, Buharum had to wonder. The slave might die any moment. He thought he saw a faint glimpse of pale bone deep in the terrible ruts gashed open on the slave's back – but maybe his imagination just ran away with him in so thick a darkness, only bright enough to allow one's imagination to run at all.

"This man is lucky to be alive," Dunewalker said. "He's a fighter. Most people would let go of life after this and end their suffering."

"Slaves hold on to what they have," Farrah commented. "Like their lives."

"Or their faith," Solon added, throwing her a look. She returned it dryly. Their eyes met for a bit too long – Buharum waved a hand between them. Unfortunately, he couldn't actually reach their gazes to break the spell, so his gesture went unnoticed.

"Blasted impressive is what it is," Kukrum muttered under his breath, still looking at the abomination's massive corpse. "Look at its gut. Had to have eaten several people before he killed it – how did it do that?"

"No doubt it was planning to eat them *all* later," Buharum added with a shudder. "Disgusting."

"We'll take over their camp for now," said Solon. "Bring the horses – and leave the beast. Its body will warn the other creatures off long enough for us to see this man healed."

"That won't be easy," said Dunewalker, already tending the slave's injuries. "If he survives, it'll be a miracle. You'd best start praying; I'll burn a sacrifice once I've sealed the wounds."

Solon wasted no time, bowing his head to rumble deep, monotone prayers in his voice like grinding stone. Despite being from the lands to the north, the region now called the Achaean Empire, Solon followed the Old Kingdom gods of Kemhet. Kukrum didn't say a word, going to fetch some more supplies for Dunewalker, while Farrah stood her ground. Buharum gently elbowed her leg to prompt her to add her own voice to their prayers, before he too began praying that no deity would yet take the slave's life.

Buharum couldn't sleep. Not only were they in the Blasted Wastes, the worst place imaginable, but the nearby ragged breathing of the dying slave resting flat on his belly kept him awake. It was the only sound for leagues, and each of the slave's labored breaths drove a unique tension into his soul.

The others managed better. Dunewalker and Solon genuinely slumbered, while Farrah and Kukrum sat wide awake, looking around in the darkness and fog with exhausted eyes.

At some point in the night, Kukrum inched over to Buharum and leaned forward into the corner of his vision. Buharum turned to his clan-brother, absently stroking his thick beard.

"Something bothering you?" Buharum asked, keeping his voice low to not wake the others.

His fellow dwarf shifted in his seat. "Many things," Kukrum replied, but he hesitated and straightened his helmet. Buharum would have to string it out of him, as usual.

"Tell me what's on your mind."

Also as usual, Kukrum launched right into it when given permission. "I'm not sure we're doing the right thing. Saving this slave – on the one hand, yes, we should save him, shouldn't we? But on the other, what if he's just as insane and cultish as the rest of them?"

Buharum gave his clan-brother a long look. "And what if he is?"

"We can't trust someone like that."

"I'm not gonna go and make tea with him, brother. He'll lead us to the fortress, that's all. I thought you wanted to help everyone, no matter what – didn't you say that once? Or... *more* than once?"

Kukrum clammed up, frowning deeply into his dark beard. "He doesn't *look* trustworthy," he muttered.

Buharum gave the slave a closer inspection, though he could hardly see him with his face flat against the bedroll. He had olive skin, black hair barely grown out from his head having been shaven before, and an impressive build for a slave. Despite clearly not being fed enough and thus being on the gangly side, he still looked reasonably strong and sturdy.

"Judging a book by its cover, even after all this time?" Buharum prompted, throwing Kukrum another look – only to find that his clan-brother had already moved off, leaving him alone. Buharum snorted and resumed waiting for the sunrise.

Hours passed, slowly and stressfully. Finally, after what felt like ages, sunlight stole through the mist. Just as Buharum sat up to check on Farrah, who hadn't moved for several hours and may have been asleep sitting up, the slave beside him caught his attention.

He was moving.

Subtly, the slave twitched. Dark blood had already soaked the recently changed bandages on the man's back – and he'd been through several bandages. The slave very slowly got his arms underneath him in an attempt to sit up. Suddenly, Dunewalker appeared to help, making the slave keep his back straight and lifting him into a sitting position.

"Easy, stranger," said Dunewalker. "I'm surprised you're still alive, much less moving on your own."

The slave didn't answer at first. Pain was etched into his face, and he pinched his eyes shut, his jaw set hard. Solon arrived next, kneeling and offering the slave a skin of drink.

"Take your time," Solon said in as gentle a tone as his voice of tumbling rocks could manage, "then tell us your name."

The slave accepted the drink – only to pause before it touched his lips, which made Buharum screw up his brow in confusion. Dunewalker, however, apparently understood. He took the skin, drank a swallow, and offered it once more. Only then did the slave accept it, gulping down its contents like his life depended on it. Which maybe it did.

"Not sure why we'd poison you after just saving your life," Buharum remarked, but Solon waved a hand at him to shut up. Buharum showed his palms and did as ordered.

After he finished drinking and gathered his wits for another moment, the slave finally spoke. "Thank you," he said, and Solon nodded.

"They call me Solon Sun-Eyes, follower of Amun-Ra. You're the only survivor of your convoy. Do you remember anything?"

At first, it almost seemed he didn't, from the way the slave's dark eyes grew distant. Buharum watched him in silence and thought on what Kukrum had said about him looking untrustworthy – but he didn't agree. This slave's features were perhaps more striking than Buharum had ever seen short of a pharaoh, befitting a high-born noble from a prestigious bloodline rather than someone of his position.

The man's nose looked like the curved beak of a royal falcon, with a sharp, dark brow that heavily shadowed his deep-set brown eyes, lending more to his raptor-like visage. His black hair had a low and pointed widow's peak to make him look all the more severe, particularly with his cheekbones high and chiseled, tapering down to a strong chin.

What told of his lack of nobility, though, was all the hair on his deep olive-gold skin. His arms and legs and chest were dusted with dark hair. A noble Kemheti and even some of the more well-kept slaves would've had no hair on their bodies – or even on their face or atop their head, much like Solon.

So too did the slave have a dark stubble on his face, as well as a small triangle of dark facial hair directly below his rather overstated lower lip, which currently looked even more prominent from his scowl. Dark sideburns reached just below his tall cheekbones.

"I remember fighting that thing," the slave answered, his eyes flicking over to the stinking corpse of the abomination he'd slain still lying not too far off, "but... not very well."

His gaze roved over each of them in turn. He lingered momentarily on Buharum and Kukrum, the latter of whom had joined them, before he looked at Farrah, then Solon and his tattoos, and finally Dunewalker.

"Two dwarves – and three humans, each from a different land," the slave observed aloud under his breath, almost dryly. "Only one group could've assembled people like you... the Medjai. So Tefnahkt finally drew your attention."

Buharum wasn't surprised that the slave had heard of their order. Perhaps what gave it away wasn't the dwarves among them but was Solon's runic tattoos. Word had long since spread across Kemhet that the Medjai were among the only people who used that dangerous magic. To see such tattoos was to know a sacred guardian of Kemhet had arrived.

"Tefnahkt?" Buharum echoed. "Tefnahkt the Red? So he *is* your master?"

"Yes," the slave replied.

"We can talk about that in a moment," Solon cut in. "What's your name?"

The slave fell quiet, as if he wasn't sure to trust them, his brow furrowing. But he answered at length, "I'm called Djedar... Djedar Rath."

Buharum couldn't help but chuckle. "*Djed*, eh? That's what you Kemhetis call Osiris's backbone. Ironic, considering yours might never be the sa—"

Solon jammed one of his massive elbows into Buharum's shoulder, almost knocking him into the sand. Buharum cleared his throat. Djedar only cut him a grim look – but then a small, wry smile played on his lips. He snorted and shook his head, looking down again as if falling deep into thought. Buharum almost grinned.

"Ah, finally, a man who appreciates irony," Buharum remarked. "Glad I can say I've met *one*. I am Buharum, and this is my clan-brother Kukrum."

Kukrum gave a shy little wave and a smile.

Dunewalker spoke next, saying, "I go by Dunewalker. And that," he motioned to the only woman present, "is Farrah, Deshreti mistress of blades."

Farrah flashed a dark smile. "Thanks for the title, Dunewalker – I've never had one before. I'll try to remember it."

Solon, however, remained focused on their mission. "If Tefnahkt is your master, can you show us where his fortress is?"

Though his strength was visibly fading, the slave Djedar nodded. But he sagged forward, his eyes falling shut. Agony and exhaustion were etched in hard lines on his handsome features. Dunewalker caught him with gentle hands and lowered him back onto the bedroll.

"*Later,*" Dunewalker said almost harshly, casting Solon a look. "He needs rest."

"Healer's orders," Buharum commented.

"Indeed."

"No— wait," Djedar said, mustering the energy to keep his eyes open. "You Medjai think you know about Tefnahkt, but he's more powerful than people claim. I've seen him – he can kill with a gesture, fill entire rooms with red fire..."

Buharum fell quiet. Much as he enjoyed making light of everything Men took too seriously and thought was the end of the world, even he knew when to stop.

"He's used it on me – on all the slaves. It doesn't burn your skin. It burns... something else."

"His magic burns your soul," Solon said. "That's what you felt. He has the powers of a demon, one he bound himself to. Do you know of the *Zharduvari?*"

Djedar weakly lifted one long, dark eyebrow in an expression Buharum couldn't read.

"The Zharduvari..."

"Or simply the Zhar," Buharum put in, but Solon kept talking.

"...are an ancient cult who believe only in the march of time – and the arrival of death, at least death of their mortal bodies. The only thing they value is power. Most make pacts with greater beings, like Tefnahkt did with a demon, and like he might seek to do with the ancient pharaoh Ankhu the Endless."

Djedar stared. "Ankhu is a myth."

Dunewalker scoffed. "If only he was."

"The Zharduvari are real, and so is Ankhu," said Solon. "His tomb was buried deep in the sand of foreign lands as punishment for his age of cruelty to the people of Kemhet. No one was ever meant to find his tomb or awaken him. The curse..."

"Are you sure you want to tell him all this?" Farrah cut in, moving closer. "How do we know he isn't playing us?"

Djedar didn't speak, his weary eyes distant, and Buharum got the distinct impression he was still trying to process all the mysticism and now-real mythology that'd just been dumped on his head. He almost felt sorry for him.

Apparently her words convinced Solon, though. "We'll discuss it more later," he said. "Get some sleep, Rath; your wounds will heal with tending and prayer. Tomorrow morning, we leave for Tefnahkt's fortress – we can't waste any more time."

"I'll help you," Djedar said, voice low and eyes shut again. "But we have to go deeper into the Wastes to reach him."

Kukrum finally had something to add. "Dangerous as it is for *anyone*, friend, traveling the Wastes is something only the Medjai and Dunewalker's people can do safely – and we have both. Don't worry about that now. Get some sleep."

Djedar didn't look convinced, but he returned to a fairly comfortable position on his bedroll again with Dunewalker's aid. Buharum, for his part, went back to sitting and losing himself in thought.

The following morning, they did exactly as Solon commanded and wasted no more time. What meager tidbits of camp they had put down were quickly taken up again, Djedar claimed the void iron black sword he had used to slay the monster, and off they went deeper into the Wastes.

Dunewalker led the way, as his people were known to walk the Blasted Wastes like no others could. Much of their civilization, the land of Axa, had been tainted by it; they fought always to maintain what ground remained. Buharum took up a place right behind him, with Kukrum still riding double like he always did. Solon allowed Djedar to share his horse, and Farrah still rode alone.

Much as he had traveled and even occasionally dared to enter these forsaken deserts, Buharum never felt at peace amidst the grey sands and the strange fog that rolled through now and then. No one *could*. Dunewalker also looked on edge, his very dark eyes looking everywhere, like he expected an ambush.

"Is it true," Farrah suddenly said, "that the Headless Men live here?"

"Many locals call them 'blemmyes,'" Dunewalker replied.

"That's a yes, then. Headless men are real."

"As real as you or I, and as real as the crocotta or whatever the beast was that attacked Djedar."

"You have a *name* for that creature?" Djedar commented. "Do you Medjai name everything?"

Dunewalker laughed. "Some of us do."

"I'm sure those headless men think we look odd, too," Kukrum put in. "Imagine seeing someone *with* a head when you don't have one. They have faces on their chests instead!"

"I 'imagine' I'd be jealous," Farrah cracked dryly. "I'd hate to see what their *women* look like."

Dunewalker made a face. "I'd not thought of that…"

Buharum, however, had to laugh. "I've seen them at a distance – the men, that is. Heard they ambush travelers sometimes, though, so we better hope we don't meet any."

Djedar finally spoke again, though his words were quiet. "The last thing I'm worried about out here is any kind of man, head or not."

Such a comment killed the conversation in a hurry. But Solon clearly didn't appreciate the silence.

"You look and sound Kemheti, Rath, and at least your first name is as well," he said. "But I think you recognized the name 'Zharduvari,' and you seem to speak the Parsanshari word like a natural. Were you born there, or near it? Or... something else?"

Djedar snorted. "Maybe I'm the crossed son of the king of kings and the pharaoh's own bloodline. There's no way to know for sure, is there?"

Solon ignored Djedar's irreverence. "You were born into slavery, then?"

"Yes," Djedar answered, finally sounding serious. "It's all I've ever known. Breaking rocks, digging sand, waiting on those who held my chains, tending to animals..." His voice drifted, his gaze growing distant as it did so often. "The animals are the kindest. The silence of the desert comes in second. As for my Parsanshari, thank you. I've been working on it."

That earned a chuckle from Solon. "I've never bothered learning. This language serves me well enough."

Djedar nodded. "Kemheti is my native tongue, but the more languages you learn, the more you know what everyone says about you."

"Well, you will be a slave no longer, my friend."

Djedar lifted a dark brow again and asked coyly, "Am I not still one right now?"

Buharum barked a laugh. "He isn't *wrong*, really…"

Ahead of them, Dunewalker held up a hand. Everyone stopped. Silence settled once again, and Buharum joined the others in looking around for whatever Dunewalker had spotted – until the Axan lowered his hand and pointed far off to their left.

"They heard you," was all Dunewalker said.

They lurked not far, like devils spoken of – tall figures with lanky limbs, almost human yet still distorted and wrong. Their large hands grasped spears ending in wicked, jagged points, with belts of still more weapons hanging around their waists. And they had no heads.

The diffused light of the sun in the fog showed only the silhouettes of the strange headless men who watched them, making them look like malformed beheaded corpses walking on two legs. Where a neck should have been was only a flat plain between their shoulders. Buharum barely made out two slight twinkles on their broad upper chests – their eyes.

"Why would the gods create such an accursed thing?" Solon muttered.

"The gods did not touch these lands after the mages had their wars," Dunewalker replied. "Those headless men, like so much else here, were twisted by arcane powers. No god meant for those to exist... That's what they say, at least."

Djedar said only, "They say a lot of things."

They remained still for a while. The headless men did the same, watching them from atop their far grey dune. A drawn-out silent challenge passed between each group, waiting to see what the other would do. Until finally the blemmyes left, their headless forms disappearing over the crest of the ashen sands.

Buharum exhaled at last and sagged forward in his saddle, earning himself a gentle pat on the shoulder from Kukrum. Meanwhile, Dunewalker finally resumed their trek.

"We are lucky," he remarked. "Maybe they like us."

"Or even *those* creatures know about the Medjai," said Farrah.

"Or," Kukrum cut in, "they aren't as evil as Men claim."

Buharum scoffed. "Curse you and your sickening kindness, brother."

"*Someone* around here has to be kind. Everyone acts so jaded."

Djedar offered yet another theory: "The headless men might be angry about Tefnahkt and his fortress."

"That seems likely, as they weren't far from it," replied Dunewalker. "Look."

A shape materialized in the mist far ahead of them: their destination. High walls reached above the unnatural desert, as grey as the sands from which they rose. Behind those walls they could just make out the top of a greater structure towering in the center: Tefnahkt's personal keep, Buharum wagered. His palace in the middle of nowhere.

"He's got an entire walled town to himself," Buharum remarked, once again stroking his enormous beard. "That's certainly not arrogant."

Djedar intoned a low, throaty hum in thought before replying, "Yes. It won't be easy getting in... I hope you Medjai have a plan."

"I think we might," Solon said, "and we also have no choice."

"I'll admit, I didn't think I'd meet the legendary Medjai only to see them acting as assassins."

Buharum wasn't offended; he was too old to take such easy offense at words. But he could almost sense the anger drop over everyone else like a shroud. Djedar caught a lot of hard stares that he stonily endured. That continued until Buharum cleared his throat.

"We're not assassins; we're guardians. Protectors."

Djedar only hummed again and nodded, not buying it at all.

"If the Zharduvar cultist in that castle wasn't a coward hiding in the middle of nowhere, we wouldn't *have* to play assassin and go after him," Farrah sniped.

The only human present whose pride didn't seem stabbed by Djedar's assassin comparison was Dunewalker, who said, "The glory days of the Medjai are long past. There was a time we would have met these opponents in honorable battle. But now we are reduced to groups as small as this, wandering the desert and enforcing law on a vast and barren land, full of evil that hides. When evil hides, good must go and seek it out."

"And killing for good is not the work of assassins," Solon finished for him.

At first, Djedar said nothing, though Buharum noticed a hint of dark amusement on his face. Buharum almost wanted to ask him to elaborate on whatever it was he found funny, but he didn't bother. No doubt the others wouldn't find it funny, anyway.

He wasn't sure he trusted their newfound friend, though.

"I'll help you get inside and show you where Tefnahkt stays," Djedar said. "I'll even help you kill him, if I can, but like I said – he has powers beyond us all."

"We'd better get moving, then," Buharum prompted, setting his horse off down the other side of the dune. "Demon or warlock, we need to reach him before the new moon."

Silence fell harder than a stone dropped in temple during a ceremony.

Oh, damn. Buharum shrank in the saddle as all eyes turned to him – especially Djedar.

"I shouldn't have said that," Buharum muttered.

"What happens on the new moon?" asked Djedar, lifting his head.

"We don't have time to explain," Farrah declared. "Let's get inside that fortress."

Night had settled over the Blasted Wastes by the time Buharum and the other Medjai approached the high outer walls of Tefnahkt's mighty fortress. They came to a halt less than a league away, attention focused fully on their destination as everyone collectively wondered how to breach even the first set of walls – much less the second, in Tefnahkt's inner keep.

Solon motioned for them to dismount, and each warrior silently lowered themselves from their steeds. Dunewalker took the horses down from atop the dune upon which they had all perched, trying to keep them out of sight, while Solon and Djedar went to give the walls yet another once-over.

Buharum stood just behind them, stroking his massive beard once again as he lost himself in thought. No one present had ever actually breached a fortress – save, perhaps, for him. He had done it so long ago with his clan-brother Kukrum by his side. That had been very different... they'd had an army and siege engines, not a team of wandering warriors.

"We can't get any bolts between *those* stones," Kukrum commented, looking wistfully at the heavy crossbow in his hands. "I don't think our and Farrah's usual tricks will work here."

"We can't assault the gates. We could try disguises..." Solon mused aloud, but Djedar spoke next.

"No one goes in or out without Tefnahkt knowing about it beforehand. There aren't any visitors in the Wastes. The slave-driver Blacksword was meant to lead our caravan – without him or at least one of his men, they wouldn't let us through."

"What about you? They know you, don't they?"

Djedar snorted. "They know me and they fear me. If I showed up without slave-drivers leading me in chains, I don't think it'd be pretty."

Dunewalker's interest was piqued. "*Fear* you?"

"Yes. You don't find me terrifying?" Djedar remarked dryly, his attention elsewhere.

"We saved your life," Farrah pointed out. "You could at least tell us what you're talking about."

"You're right," replied Djedar, "but I'd like to hear more about what *you're* not telling me first. Like why you care about the new moon, the story of Ankhu, and those pictures of the gods on the walls of that tomb... What exactly is Tefnahkt hoping to find?"

No one answered him, proving his point in a way that made Buharum shuffle awkwardly on his feet. Not telling Djedar about the ancient tale of Ankhu was one thing – like Farrah said, could they really trust him? And yet, he also felt it wrong to lead this man around without him knowing exactly what he was getting into.

Solon scowled, crossing his thick, muscular arms – and then his hard expression melted. His gaze landed upon something barely visible, concealed at a far side of the fortress.

"Does the town have a sewer system?" he asked.

Djedar blinked. "You won't get in like that. The pipes aren't big enough."

A rare smile played on Solon's lips as he regarded Buharum and Kukrum and said, "We won't need it to be big enough for *us*."

Buharum's mind crashed to a halt, and he made a show of very slowly turning his head before looking all the way up at the faces of Solon and Djedar. Both regarded the two short dwarves, their Medjai captain wearing a confident smile and their newly freed slave friend looking pensive, as he so often did.

Kukrum gave Buharum a nudge on the shoulder, but Buharum smacked his hand away. Hard.

"I'm not crawling through a sewer," Buharum said firmly. "You want someone to do that, find yourself another Besak – or a *very* small Man."

"I have two Besak-ha right here," Solon replied, amused, "and they're under *my* command."

"Curse you for the Medjai putting you in charge," Buharum grumbled, puffing himself up. "I'll never get the smell out of my beard..."

Meanwhile, Kukrum put on a stupid grin, teeth shining through his own copious facial hair. "Brother, aren't you the one who's supposed to make the jokes?"

"Not when there's shit involved. Actual feces. I plan to live for another good hundred-some years, not die of a plague because I waded through a sewer like an idiot."

"You're saving the world, Buharum," Farrah put in sweetly. But Farrah was never sweet, Buharum knew that, so he only rolled his eyes.

"Not worth it. At least I'd die without having to crawl through the dung of a bunch of brainwashed humans all wanting to live together in the middle of a wasteland."

"Dung-beetles are holy," Solon said, giving Buharum a hard clap on the shoulder that made him wince. "Think of it as a test from Ra."

Buharum scoffed, muttering under his breath, "I'll see to it that Bes has a word with the Sun King about putting his servants through such humiliation, all just because we're *short*. And maybe I'll give you a ball of poo afterward to offer to Ra, Solon."

Kukrum, smiling stupidly, gave Buharum some consoling pats on the back while he spied the sewer grate in question. "I'm sure we can fit. Don't worry, Buharum will come around by the time we get down there."

"I know he will," Solon said with a chuckle. "Gods watch over you two."

Buharum made a face and mimed Solon's words, but he threw his hands in the air and said, "Fine! We'll get inside, but how does that help? We can't go throw the main gates open wide. They'll kill us and have us for supper or something. I don't know what these cultists are fed."

The mention of food made everyone fall quiet. Their supplies had grown thinner each day they'd traveled, and with the extra man and having to tend to his wounds, food and drink in particular had been rationed beyond reason. Barely a moment later, someone's stomach grumbled a loud enough complaint that it made Buharum search for the culprit. He found Djedar's brows had become tightly knit, like he staved off hunger-nausea.

"Tefnahkt *doesn't* eat people, right?" Buharum threw over his shoulder.

"What? No. Tefnahkt might be a cultist, but he isn't inhuman," Djedar said, barely paying him any attention; Buharum was just happy to get a straight answer. Then Djedar pointed at the far eastern side of the fortress. "There's a postern gate not far from the stables on the eastern side, beyond our view from here. It shouldn't be hard to access from one of the larger sewer grates. If you can get that open, I can lead everyone else inside."

"Looked around a lot at the fortress's insides, haven't you?" commented Farrah. "Planning an escape?"

Djedar offered a smile Buharum could only interpret as mysterious. "Something like that."

"We'll find you there," Solon said.

Buharum scoffed. "You'd better. And now I'll go wade through shit."

With that, they got moving. Kukrum led the way, chipper as ever, throwing Buharum an optimistic smile as they walked. A quick assessment of the walls high above, however, revealed a silhouetted shape overlooking the desert. Only one, though. The walls kept out beasts, and imagining intruders of human intelligence approaching a fortress in the Wastes was preposterous.

Still, Tefnahkt's sheer overconfidence continued to surprise.

Buharum and Kukrum hunkered down briefly, long enough for Buharum to prepare his crossbow, hoping they hadn't been seen—

An arrow, little more than a thin line of black against the dark of night, flew from nowhere and lodged directly in the figure on the walls. Buharum saw the watchman crumple and collapse, and the dwarves resumed their trek.

"I wonder if that was Solon or Dunewalker. I suppose it could've been either, but Solon's aim has never ceased to amaze me," Kukrum said. "I suppose that's why they call him Sun-Eyes. No wonder he's a captain, even among the Medjai. Have you ever seen him miss his mark, brother? I'd love to see him and Dune have a competition sometime. They're both incredible..."

Buharum didn't care about offering sugary praise of either Solon or Dunewalker's exceptional archery skills. "Somebody better reward me for this," he muttered as they neared the towering grey walls. At the base of the massive structure of stone, a grated opening letting foul-smelling water run out into a trench. He turned his nose up at it, but Kukrum headed over without hesitation.

Putting his crossbow away, Kukrum took out a hammer and chisel and set to work carefully dislodging the grate from the stone around it. Buharum joined him without a word, using his own identical tools. Soon they pulled the grate out and set it aside.

The smell blasting them in the face made them both freeze. Buharum thought he felt his insides recoil in horror. Kukrum finally wore a look of apprehension, fidgeting with his massive beard. Buharum couldn't help but throw him a smug glance.

"You didn't seem worried about that beard earlier, clan-brother."

"*Every* Besak is worried about his beard," Kukrum replied instantly. "What is Bes himself without his beard, much less his servants?"

But they fell silent. One last deep breath of fresh air finally gave Buharum the courage needed to take the plunge. He stepped down into the canal of waste-water, which reached about to his belt, and started wading forward. The sewer opening was small enough that he had to crunch a bit to fit, but fit he did. Looked like Solon's plan would actually work.

Dim shafts of light showed them the way as they went, shining up ahead from more grates. Their path became a pitch-dark tunnel with only a few dismal beacons ahead. The smell was overwhelming, the stench of filth so strong it made Buharum's vision spin. He pulled his precious beard up over his nose and kept pushing forward.

Finally, they reached one of the overhead grates. Buharum paused below it, looking up the small shaft forming the most open space they had found yet in the tunnel. Kukrum arrived behind him in silence, wordlessly helping Buharum up. Drawing out his hammer and chisel again, Buharum set to work breaking a lock that held the grate in place before he pushed it aside and climbed out.

Fresh air hit him in the face. He breathed deep of the distant smell of horse and other animals, closing his eyes and reveling in anything other than the stench of waste for all of half a second before helping Kukrum also free himself from the sewer.

Now the two of them stood in an open street, prompting them to drag the grate back into place and hurry over to the shadows of a nearby sandstone building. Very few walked the streets at this hour, so with any luck, no one had noticed the appearance of the two dwarves.

The town within the walls appeared deceptively ordinary for something that stood beyond the border of the Blasted Wastes. A handful of stone buildings, most squat but with one a bit taller nearby, were arranged in neat streets surrounding the massive keep in which

Tefnahkt himself made his home. No regular patrols walked the streets like in a proper city, but Buharum still noted a handful of armed men wandering about, scattered, without exact patterns.

"No discipline," Buharum chided half-jokingly, keeping his voice low.

Kukrum shushed him and flapped his hand chidingly. Buharum made a face at him. The two quickly spotted the small postern gate set at the base of the fortifications: a simple, narrow, stone entranceway with a door of thick, matching rock to make it blend in. One half-asleep guard was posted there, leaning against the wall.

"They'll smell us a league away," Kukrum disparaged under his breath. Buharum didn't answer, but Kukrum then added, "It's a shame we have to hurt the poor sods..."

Buharum scoffed. "Is it? They're mad cultists, Kukrum. You're lamenting hurting them even though they willfully work for a man who wants to unleash evil like Ankhu?"

Kukrum frowned.

Again Buharum rolled his eyes, removing his crossbow from his back and putting a bolt to the sticking place. "If you don't want to hurt the fool, then go get the door open. I'll handle him."

Looking grateful, Kukrum nodded and set off. Buharum made his way through the shadows, staying close to the buildings – not that the guard paid much attention. Maybe Tefnahkt should have told his people to better prepare for a potential attack... though at the same time, Buharum was again thankful for his arrogance.

The shadow of the building made a decent hiding place from which to aim, and Buharum lined up his shot. Across the way, he barely made out Kukrum creeping toward the postern gate.

The guard stirred. He scrunched up his nose as if he'd smelled something foul, eyes fixing immediately on the sewer grate down the street – the stench of the sewer had given them away after all.

Buharum loosed his crossbow bolt. It struck the man directly in the throat, silencing his voice as he clawed at his bleeding neck, gurgling and collapsing in an unsightly heap. Kukrum made an awful face but moved past the thrashing body. Meanwhile, Buharum arrived to show a piece of mercy and execute the guard.

The instant Kukrum pulled open the postern gate, the other Medjai appeared with Djedar in the lead. His eyes darted over the dead guard in silence. Solon followed next, giving the corpse a look and muttering a quiet prayer.

Farrah, however, spit on his corpse in a uniquely unladylike manner. Buharum winced.

"She lost her parents and most of her tribe to the Zhar," Solon said bluntly, throwing her a disapproving look. Kemheti were generally sensitive about disrespecting the dead, Imperial-born or not.

"That's personal," Farrah snapped.

Djedar, however, just shrugged. "I understand any hatred for them." He gave a jerk of his head for them to follow. "Come. Let's put the horses in the stable for now – there's plenty of room. We can come get them after we take care of Tefnahkt."

"If we survive it," Dunewalker added darkly.

"We will," said Solon with all the confidence of a fact. "The gods are on our side. And everything that happens, happens only by their design."

"Keep telling yourself that, Solon," Farrah sniped.

"Even those headless men we saw exist for a reason."

But Djedar said, "And even the gods are victims of Fate. Shai can't be denied."

'Shai.' Buharum crossed his arms; the Kemheti were obsessed with their personification of Fate itself sometimes, as so many mortals always were. Not that Buharum couldn't be fatalist, but at least he wasn't openly grim about it.

Whatever fate was in store, they made their way to the stables. Djedar reached them first, throwing open a side door and helping them lead their horses inside. Buharum entered last, trying to keep an eye on the dark and dismal streets for any signs of trouble.

Djedar struck a small flame, lighting a candle in a wall sconce like he'd done it thousand times. Even such meager light let Buharum see that the stables held a few horses other than their own, which Farrah and Dunewalker and Kukrum put in stalls for the time being.

Of more interest were the other animals. A camel watched from a far stall, and a shrill shriek overhead made Buharum start out of his skin.

Djedar chuckled, a low and chesty sound that made something in the back of Buharum's mind want to think of him as a villain. The former slave wrapped a cloth around one arm, lifted it, then gave a short whistle – and down from the rafters flew a beautiful falcon, landing perfectly on his hand.

He fed the bird a scrap of meat he'd apparently gotten from somewhere in the stables and said, "Tefnahkt's prize falcon. He claims it can find him anywhere, if ordered... and finding loyalty in a falcon is a rare thing. Wouldn't surprise me if he put some kind of spell on it, the way animals usually treat him."

Next, Djedar turned and made his way to the biggest stall in the building. It housed an occupant larger than any stable beast Buharum had ever seen: an elephant. The great animal watched them in total silence, its dusty tan-grey hide crisscrossed with a few battle scars. Its massive pair of polished ivory tusks gleamed in the meager candlelight, the ends adorned with sheaths of gold covered in intricate designs. Other jewelry besides decorated its head and hide, not removed even when the animal was at rest. Beady eyes set amidst a helping of wrinkles gleamed somehow brighter than the ornamentations, lighting up at Djedar's approach.

The Kemheti slave went to the animal like an old friend, murmuring a few soothing words. The elephant sauntered closer, slowly and gently, lifting its long trunk in greeting to touch Djedar's outstretched hand.

Solon, and everyone else, stared. A few of them exchanged looks.

"Impressive," Solon said. "They seem to trust you implicitly. These are the animals you spoke of?"

"Yes," replied Djedar. "I've taken care of them for years." He snorted. "They know me better than the man who is supposedly their master." But he regarded the Medjai with a critical look in his shadowed eyes, not unlike those of the falcon on his arm. "Even if this place is emptier than it used to be, we shouldn't walk around openly. There should be some spare traveling cloaks in here – find them and put them on."

While everyone spread out to search the stables, Buharum pointed out, "We need food before we fight. Or, well, I suppose we don't *need* it, but it sure would be nice."

"We *are* in a stable full of animals..." Farrah said thoughtfully.

"We don't have time for cooking," Dunewalker replied flatly.

"And these aren't beasts for slaughter," Djedar added almost in a snarl, even more of his white teeth showing than usual. Farrah shrugged and showed her hands. "There's a tavern near here. We can go there, get food... no one will ask too many questions if we don't make ourselves obvious. Each of you could easily be one of Tefnahkt's slaves, except for Solon, with those tattoos. But," he fixed Buharum and Kukrum with his dark gaze, "Tefnahkt has never had any Besak-ha loyal to him. He's tried, but none have ever turned. The two of you are going to stand out."

Buharum put on a crafty smile. "Of course he hasn't had any Besak-ha. We dwarves are righteous and holy. Good-hearted by nature, you see; we'd never serve the Zharduvari. We were made this way."

Dunewalker, naturally, had to comment. "No one is made perfect, and the Zhar can turn most anyone."

"Whatever." Buharum motioned Kukrum over. "Come here, brother. I'll sacrifice my dignity for this mission – get on my shoulders and put that cloak around us."

Kukrum blinked. "You'll embarrass our entire bloodlines. And can you even hold me up like that?"

"Of course I can; now get to it. Or would you rather I stand on *your* head?"

That got him moving. Kukrum clambered up onto Buharum's shoulders. He held his clan-brother's ankles in place, and Kukrum unfurled a cloak long enough for a man, wrapping it around his shoulders. Buharum couldn't see the result, but if he had to guess—

"You look deformed," Farrah declared with all the consideration of a cudgel. "You're too tall and your arms are too short."

Dunewalker, meanwhile, just laughed. This prompted Djedar to give another of his own villainous-sounding laughs, and even Solon chuffed out a short chuckle. Buharum's cheeks grew warm, and he was grateful no one could see him blush.

"It'll do," Solon said. "Let's go to that tavern, Rath, but we need to be quick about eating. If Tefnahkt really is that close to getting into those ruins, we don't have much time."

Djedar nodded, but he said, "We have just enough time for you to tell me what the hell is going on."

Clad in their cloaks and hoods, Djedar led the Medjai into the tavern without a problem, and an exhausted slave served them some simple meat and nutritious beer. Most *every* meal was meat and beer to keep the slaves lean and strong, capable of the hard work they had to perform.

Kukrum didn't seem to understand the food of slaves. He looked around as if in search of a side or at least bread before passing a chunk of meat under the table to Buharum, who hid there. Everyone else ate quietly.

"We owe you an explanation," said Solon, drawing all attention – and more than one outraged stare. "It isn't something we generally share with someone who isn't a Medjai sworn into our order."

"And it shouldn't be," Farrah added pointedly.

Solon gave her a nod of acknowledgment, then went on: "It also isn't something well understood. That being said, you wondered what exactly Tefnahkt is after. I'll tell you what we know…

"Tales are still bandied about of Pharaoh Ankhu the Endless, God-King, Demon-Sired, High Priest of the Black Temple. Those were only a few of his many titles. No one knows who he was before he arose as Ankhu and called himself a divine being, saying he had been chosen of Set. Ankhu said he was a union between holy and unholy: a man born of a demon now blessed with the powers of a god.

"And what power he had. He was said to summon plagues of insects from another world and to shape the very sands of the desert, like Set himself. No one remembers how exactly he was defeated. Everyone has a different story; some say the gods stepped in, some say even Set regretted what he'd done and stripped Ankhu of his power... Others claim his own sheer power overwhelmed him."

Djedar steepled his fingers in thought, staring down at the table around which they sat. It was a lot to take in. Why would the gods – any of them, even Set – be a part of a mortal wielding such reckless power? It would upset the balance of things.

He asked, "What happened after Ankhu was defeated?"

"His heart was ripped from his body, but he did not die. He was mummified alive, cursed, restricted from passing into any afterlife thanks to the removal of his heart. The heart, they say, was put in a canopic jar and hidden somewhere in his tomb. Without it, Anubis will not judge him, and his soul will never rest. He lingers forever as an undead abomination in Deshret, outside his homeland, in disgrace and punishment. The gods themselves buried his labyrinthian tomb deep in the red sands.

"Now Ankhu rises on the night of each new moon, when the power of the gods is weakest and darkness is strongest. He walks his tomb in search of the heart he will never find, as he has for a thousand years. His heart is close enough to be heard beating, they say, and that torments him – because he can never reach it." Solon shrugged one thick shoulder. "Not even the Medjai know where his heart might rest in the maze... or what kind of other torments the gods have inflicted upon him there."

Djedar scowled. The new moon...

"The new moon is almost here," Djedar said. "That's why Tefnahkt is so desperate to open the tomb. He wants Ankhu to be awake."

Solon gave a solemn nod. "And if he is freed, he will once again plague all of Kemhet as an unstoppable evil. Perhaps Tefnahkt wants to make a deal with him, somehow gain his power... or else, serve him. The Zharduvari will no doubt want to convert him to their cult. It doesn't matter, though, what he wants – we can't let it happen. If he awakens the mummy, there will be no stopping him— not without his heart."

"Your master," said Dunewalker, pulling Djedar's attention to him instead, "must find a way into that tomb *this* new moon, or the Medjai will stop him. He knows this. He cannot wait another month. Whatever he was doing to prepare, such as trying to find the heart first – none of that matters to him now."

Djedar swallowed. He lifted his head, eyes distant. "There is another who knows about the tomb. Meresamun, Tefnahkt's favorite consort. She even knows about this fortress. What more than that she knows, I can't be sure, but... she came by the dig site only a few nights ago."

The Medjai present exchanged several significant looks before Farrah said, "Meresamun is the name of a high-born noblewoman in Waset, one of Kemhet's most important cities. You're *sure* it's her?"

"If the Zharduvari already have people in positions like that, they're better at playing this game than we thought," Solon muttered.

Djedar arched a long, dark brow. "She got much more... *personal* than Tefnahkt. I got a good look at her. If I ever saw her again, I could tell you for certain, but I know what she said: she claimed her name was

Meresamun and said she was leaving to go back to Waset." He shrugged. "That's all I know. Now... how are we getting into that keep?"

Of all people, Farrah put on an uncharacteristic smile. "Leave that to me."

Farrah stayed close to Buharum and Kukrum as they approached the keep in the center of Tefnahkt's walled town. Djedar led the way, like usual, casting continual glances back at them. Farrah always evenly met each look, wondering why he seemed so concerned about keeping a close eye on everyone.

Still, he led them true. They approached the base of the keep's walls—

Djedar stopped, held out an arm, and backed up. Kukrum and Buharum halted so abruptly that they nearly came crashing down in their ridiculous disguise.

Two warriors led a cart, pulled by a weary slave, down the street ahead. Djedar looked back at the Medjai long enough to press a finger to his lips for silence.

The guards took no interest in them, their attention focused on their assignment – dumping dead bodies, from the look of it. When the cart rattled by, Farrah moved forward to peer at its contents: two corpses in a mess of gangly limbs. The bodies had no heads...

"Blemmyes," Dunewalker murmured. "Tefnahkt kills them?"

"He occasionally makes a show of killing a creature from the Wastes," Djedar answered as he resumed leading the way. "He does it to keep all his followers in line – to keep them thinking that he's a living god. He's lost many of his people to his performances of power. He's the only one who stands a chance against the things out there."

They came to a halt at the base of the keep's high wall. Djedar craned his neck looking up, pushing the hood off his head. Solon did the same, but instead of looking thoughtful, he addressed the two dwarves.

"Buharum," he ordered, "time to shed that disguise."

"With pleasure," Buharum's muffled voice answered as Kukrum climbed down off his shoulders, tossing the robe aside. Buharum removed the hefty crossbow from his back, loading in a bolt and moving farther back again. Farrah followed him.

Meanwhile, Djedar watched with interest. "You look like you've done this before."

"They have," replied Dunewalker.

"Practiced on the walls at various Medjai outposts, at least," Buharum said with a wry smile. "I'll try to make them even this time, Farrah. Wouldn't want you slipping and falling; the world might end."

"Your jokes aren't very funny when that might actually happen, Buharum," Solon chided.

The dwarf shrugged. "*I* think so."

Then he lifted his crossbow and took aim for the cracks between the sandstone blocks composing Tefnahkt's personal fortress. The first bolt shot straight into a crack and stuck fast. Buharum reloaded without wasting a moment, filling the wall with bolts all the way up to an open walkway on the side of the keep, overlooking the streets below.

Farrah watched silently, gauging the distance between each bolt. She nudged Buharum once he was done, pointing to a large gap between one set of bolts, so he added another.

All the while, Djedar watched with his brow furrowed. Farrah wondered if he understood – and then he remarked, "You must be a skilled climber."

"Very," Solon replied, wearing a small smile and cutting his bright eyes her way. Farrah puffed herself up so as not to blush, while Kukrum passed her a long rope ladder.

"Don't go anywhere," she said as she approached the wall – and started to climb.

First one bolt, then the next. She pulled herself up with ease and grace, her light weight making the strong bolts of Besaki design hardly budge from their place wedged expertly between the stones. Buharum's aim had never let her down for this particular trick.

But as she made her way up along the wall, her mind wandered. Her tribe had always admonished her for her interest in things like climbing, knife-fighting, and even dancing. And when the Zharduvari had come to wipe out her people, all her knife tricks and acrobatics could do nothing. The Medjai had saved what was left... and they had been so few.

Farrah neared the top, pulling herself from so many bad memories. Grabbing hold of the ledge, she peered over the edge, looking up and down the open walkway in search of guards, but there were none.

She pulled herself up, hefting the rope ladder from her shoulder and anchoring it to a stone handrail along the edge. She tossed it over and waited, looking down at the silhouetted shapes of her companions gathering at the dangling ladder.

Voices drifted up, and she strained to listen. Djedar hesitated. He seemed to be having trouble due to the injuries to his back, so others went before him. Solon came first and climbed quickly, soon hauling his large, muscular form up over the railing and regarding her with another of his charming smiles.

"Good work," he said, and again Farrah fought a blush. She merely nodded, pretending to be very interested in their companions' progress up the ladder.

"What's happening?" she asked.

"Rath is having some trouble climbing, but he should be fine. Dunewalker will help him. He's better with wounds than I."

Farrah snorted. "He and Buharum both. Ironic that Dunewalker's a healer now, given he said he used to be a killer."

"We've *all* killed, and he never said 'killer.' All he said was he was once a warrior and set himself down a path of redemption for his own reasons."

"Nobody wants redemption that badly unless they took a life. Or several lives..."

"He feels guilt for what happens to most of our channelers, I know, although it wasn't his fault. But we shouldn't assume. He never talks about his past, even when maybe he should." Solon quirked a brow at her. "Very much like someone else."

The other Medjai began to arrive, giving Farrah a chance to dismiss Solon's jab with a wave of her hand. Buharum and Kukrum came up first, one after the other, inseparable as always. Next came Djedar, climbing the ladder slowly, underhanded. Dunewalker arrived behind him, apparently having watched to make sure he didn't fall.

"You do well for a man with a damaged spine," Dunewalker remarked, a flash of white smile showing against his very dark skin. "Being adaptable is an important part of being a Medjai."

Djedar shook his head. "I'm no Medjai."

"Not *yet*."

"I'm not sure the man wants to run around risking his neck for nobody in particular and get no recognition for it, having been a slave for so long," Buharum remarked. "Most value their freedom more than we do."

"I've never known freedom," Djedar replied. "If we take down Tefnahkt, I'd like a taste of it before I even consider what comes next."

"Our life as Medjai requires us to find satisfaction in our thankless work," said Solon. "That's why there are so few of us now... Show us where to go, Rath."

Djedar nodded and gestured them to follow with a jab of his strong chin. They soon reached a door and entered a hall that took Farrah's breath away.

Lavish and beautiful, it didn't look like anything one would find in the Blasted Wastes. Gold and burgundy gilded the walls while a long, plush rug of Parsanshari design spanned the stretch of the long corridor, which was lined with unlit candles in sconces, open triangular windows looking out into the night, and an occasional mosaic decorating the walls.

Those mosaics, however, depicted nothing beautiful. Images of demons and dark magic twisted in incomprehensible shapes on the walls. A pair of pale blue-white eyes stared out from a shadowy nothing that extended black tendrils toward the viewer. The living dead walked under an inky black, starless sky, across the rolling dunes of the desert, a half-destroyed pyramid silhouetted behind them. Runes that Farrah could not read dotted each sconce...

"A mortal man depicting things such as this," Solon muttered, "is a man whose soul could not possibly be saved."

"Every soul *could* be saved, but they don't always want it," Dunewalker retorted quietly.

"You're banking on that, aren't you, Dunewalker?" Buharum remarked as if trying to lighten the mood. It didn't work.

"Men don't take joking about their souls very well, brother," Kukrum chided.

Dunewalker pulled in a slow breath and sniped, "I was a great man once, or so everyone said. But I was not a *good* man, and that's what matters. If Tefnahkt would seek redemption, he might find it – but he never will."

The finality in Djedar's smooth, deep voice affected each of them when he spoke next. "It's up to him whether he begs Anubis for mercy when we find our vengeance. Don't start thinking he can be saved. He can't."

The next door they reached made Djedar hesitate. He pointedly drew the black-bladed khopesh on his side. Everyone else followed suit, readying their weapons.

"Leave the warlock for me," said Solon. "I'm the only one who can survive his power."

One of Djedar's long, dark eyebrows lifted, and his shadowed eyes cut in Solon's direction. "He's no weakling. I don't know what power you think you have over him, but don't put too much faith in it."

Solon held up an arm, showing some of his many black, pointed, and sweeping tattoos. "No power will defeat these. Dunewalker's people long ago mastered the art of turning magic back on its wielder, and long ago this became a power passed to the Medjai captains."

"It's not easily or lightly given," Dunewalker added darkly.

Djedar didn't look impressed; his gaze swept over those myriad tattoos only once before he lifted his head and said, "Just don't get yourself killed."

Solon offered a confident smile – *too* confident. Farrah prodded him hard in his ribs, but she may as well have tried poking a brick wall.

Though the previous room was lavish, the next they entered surpassed it. Farrah had never seen the mighty temples of Kemhet or Parsanshar, but she imagined only they could compare to something of this grandeur. Arched windows reached almost the height of the walls themselves on either side of the chamber. Starlight spilled over the floor, the only illumination; every sconce along the pillars in the vast, open room was unlit. The wind billowed inward the long curtains of pure pale silk that seemed to glow in the night.

The intricacy almost overwhelmed her senses. Everything was beautiful, if even in a disturbing way, from the delicate hatched panes of the windows to the interlocked colors of the perfectly smooth, shimmering mosaics of Ahriman, Parsanshari god of darkness and evil, and distorted demons that spread over the entirety of the floor. Complimenting the mosaic were busts of Kemheti animal-headed gods and twisted demons protruding from the sides of the room's columns, as if Tefnahkt was determined to encompass almost every religion in the Far South in this chamber alone.

Yet despite those few Kemheti depictions, the architecture and general mood and feel of the structure was distinctly Parsanshari. Tefnahkt was clearly a worldly man, given his name was one from the Black Land, not the other distant empire. What stretched out before them was a strange combination of cultures like none she had ever encountered, even in the varied peoples among the Medjai.

"For a warlock," Solon murmured under his breath, "he doesn't fear surrounding himself with gods."

"Only those gods who might not punish him," Djedar pointed out, motioning to a nearby bust. Farrah recognized it instantly – the strange visage of Set, god of chaos, his head not an ordinary animal like other gods of Kemhet. He represented himself as a red beast from the Wastes with tall, pointed ears and a long, drooping muzzle.

At the far end of the vast space rested a throne fit for a king, atop a small set of stairs... but it was empty. No guards patrolled or stood on watch, and no Tefnahkt presided.

Djedar surveyed the room before jabbing his chin over to a small door on the far side of the deathly silent chamber. Farrah let her attention linger on the oddly simple wooden throne in the otherwise pompous space.

Then the door flew open.

In stepped a bronze-skinned Kemheti man clad in a flowing regalia of burgundy robes embroidered in gold, clean-shaven but wearing a metal false beard on his chin, as often seen on pharaohs. His hands, covered in rings, were folded calmly before him as he spoke to a servant walking by his side. Three armed and armored slave-drivers trailed in his wake.

They halted, and so did the Medjai. Time seemed to stop.

First, Tefnahkt's eyes landed on Djedar, full of dark recognition. Then he looked at Solon, then Dunewalker, Buharum, Kukrum, and finally at Farrah. He saw the weapons in their hands and their tense, battle-ready stances.

Everyone moved the same instant.

Djedar gave a bloodthirsty snarl as he charged. The servant by Tefnahkt's side tried to run. Tefnahkt raised his hand, a deep red glow forming from nothing in his palm – and Solon leapt in front of it.

A blast of crimson wisps that barely constituted light, rather some indescribable form of colored darkness, flew forth from Tefnahkt's hand and straight into Solon's bared chest. He didn't balk. The red magic flowed into the countless black tattoos on his bare skin, filling him – and he lifted his own hands to launch it right back.

Even as he did, Solon shouted, "Farrah, Rath – the guards! Dune, Buharum, Kukrum – seal the chamber!"

Djedar needed no orders. Already his black blade swung through the air to slice open the throat of the slave who had tried to escape, sending him to the floor, reeling and twitching. Blood painted the beautiful stonework at their feet.

Farrah raced to help him, dual daggers in hand, while Dunewalker motioned Buharum and Kukrum to some of the various entrances of the chamber. A slave-driver rushed Farrah, swinging an axe with a crescent head. She danced aside, then leapt forward before the man could recover his momentum. She plunged her blades deep into his ribs on either side of his body, a ghastly breathless sound leaving his throat.

Kicking off from him and yanking her daggers free, Farrah whirled away from the next guard who came forward – but something struck her from behind, landing a hard blow on her arm and knocking her off-balance. Both opponents rushed to finish her off, only for Djedar to leap between them, his black khopesh carving one man in the chest with all the strength of an axe.

Blades rang through the chamber. Heavy wooden bars crashed loudly over the doors when the others sealed the exits— but still she heard the voices of Solon and the warlock himself, Tefnahkt the Red.

"So, the Medjai found me at last," Tefnahkt said over the confusion, pacing, hands open by his sides, since he needed no physical weapons. "After so long of searching – so much wasted time. Are you truly tomb guardians, come to keep me from Ankhu's labyrinth?"

"You don't understand the evil you would unleash," Solon answered, his voice perfectly even. "The spirit of Ankhu, whatever he's become, would never serve you."

Tefnahkt barked a laugh. "I have my own plans for Ankhu and his power – I care nothing for the tales spun by your dying order to strike fear into those seeking his resting place!"

Farrah could only listen, focused as she was on the battle at hand. Though Djedar had briefly slowed one slave-driver, the other still stood strong, deflecting Djedar's every strike. Farrah came at their foe from behind, jumping up onto his tall back and driving a dagger into his neck.

He toppled like a statue, his flailing useless as she twisted the blade and put an end to his struggle. Djedar returned his attention to the remaining guard, and Farrah looked up once more – just in time to see Tefnahkt and Solon's duel come to a head.

Every blast of dark power Tefnahkt sent at Solon, his tattoos absorbed, and he cast it back. But each time, Tefnahkt deflected with a wave of his hand. They paced in broad circles over the open chamber, Tefnahkt's robes flowing behind him like bloodstained water. No one gained any ground.

Until, finally, Tefnahkt drew himself up – and threw both open hands outward. Solon spread his feet, bracing himself as if for a physical impact. It wasn't enough.

Twisted crimson energy filled every corner of the room, not a true light but not darkness, either. It had its own strange glow but didn't touch the shadows in the farthest corners, instead seeming only to turn their darkness inward and strengthen it. Tendrils of pure power sprang forth from Tefnahkt's hands, hitting Solon square in the chest— and it didn't stop.

Flame erupted from Tefnahkt's eyes, turning them to burning pits. He bared his crooked teeth and poured himself into his black magic. Solon's every tattoo filled with the otherworldly crimson hue, emitting deep red smoke. Yet still he stood his ground.

Tefnahkt focused still more, leaning forward, both hands pressed together to condense his power and focus it solely on Solon. The red smoke had a light of its own, a terrible dim glow, a disturbing light that brought no sense of comfort like a candle's welcoming flame. All the while, Tefnahkt's own flesh lost its bronze cast, his once noble appearance rapidly fading into a hideous and pale visage.

The demon was taking Tefnahkt's soul in exchange for this great use of power – neither of them could keep this up for long.

His face a mask of pain, Solon grimaced, his legs buckling. He fell to his hands and knees before he began to crumple, his body barely visible for the riling crimson smoke and red magic filling his black markings.

Only then did she realize Djedar had been right. Solon never stood a chance.

"Solon!"

Farrah called his name as she ran forward, knives ready to strike. Solon moved only enough to lift a trembling hand to stop her – but Farrah did not stop. Across the chamber, the other Medjai rushed to join them.

"Did you think your pathetic runes could stand against me!?" Tefnahkt shouted, voice distorted and booming like thunder, every word doubled as if another, unseen being spoke in tandem.

They didn't reach him in time— but a black blade soared through the air, swinging like a thrown axe. It struck Tefnahkt in the shoulder hard enough to shatter his focus.

The warlock staggered, blood darkening his robe, but the blow did little real damage. He quickly recovered, lifting his hands once more and straightening his curved spine that had been contorted like one of a possession victim. The Medjai, including Farrah, closed in around their adversary...

A blast knocked them all from their feet – but it came from Solon, not Tefnahkt.

A ripple of power and heat distorted the floor, cracking the stonework. A shockwave spreading outward, powerful enough to send every one of them sprawling to their backs. Stars briefly filled Farrah's vision when her skull smacked hard into the mosaic underfoot.

Suddenly, the first rays of dawn dared to intrude through one of the far windows. Tefnahkt hissed a curse.

"Would that I had time to kill *you* in particular, slave!" Tefnahkt snarled as he swept from the room, making his way to the far, tall doors. With a single blast of magic, he destroyed the barricade Dunewalker had set up. He disappeared into the halls before any of the Medjai had even found their footing again.

Collecting her wits, Farrah scrambled to sit upright. She didn't look where Tefnahkt had gone, nor did she pay attention to the shouts ringing through the fortress halls. She just cared about Solon... or what was left of him.

He lay crumpled on the ground, curled into a fetal position, head tucked close to his chest. Smoke still rose from his body, his skin singed all over. Distortions marred his flesh outward from some of his many tattoos, several of which looked like scars that held none of their black coloration from before.

Dunewalker hauled himself forward to stop by Solon's side, but he didn't touch him, open hands hovering just above his skin. He murmured something in a language Farrah did not understand, his brow furrowed. Solon's chest rose uneasily and only barely.

"He is alive," Dunewalker said, "but he won't be for long."

"What do we do?" Farrah blurted.

More shouting filled the hallways. Voices came toward them along with the clank of metal armor and singing of swords leaving their sheaths. Tefnahkt's men were coming. And while he didn't have a standing army, he still had more than enough men to easily overwhelm their little group.

"We can't stay here," Kukrum blurted, while Buharum silently reloaded his crossbow. The Besak gave Solon a once-over before declaring, "We have to leave him."

"What!?" Farrah shouted.

"It's what he would want," Kukrum replied. "It's for the greater good – our mission is Tefnahkt. Solon would have gladly given himself to see him stopped, and so he did."

"Harsh, brother," muttered Buharum, "especially for you."

Dunewalker rose to his feet, towering over Kukrum. "We will *not* leave him – we'll carry him as he would any of us!"

Farrah didn't bother answering Kukrum, gingerly sliding a hand under Solon's nearest heavy, muscular arm and saying, "Someone help me get him up—"

"They're coming, and they'll be too many!" Kukrum retorted. "We can't carry Solon out of here *and* fight our way out, and we *must* survive at least long enough to stop Tefnahkt!"

She didn't expect it, but Djedar suddenly came to her aid.

"We can and we will," said Djedar, retrieving his black blade and returning it to his belt. He scarcely seemed bothered by the guards almost on top of them as he knelt to help her lift Solon; Farrah could scarcely budge him on her own. "All of you, follow me – I have a plan."

Dunewalker took Djedar's place in assisting Farrah with Solon's limp, unconscious form, letting Djedar lead the way once more, to the back side of Tefnahkt's great hall. The other Medjai hurried after him, with Kukrum casting frequent fervent glances at the open doors. But Djedar stopped for nothing, reaching the entrance Tefnahkt himself had used. It opened into a hallway that felt cramped in comparison to the vast chamber from before.

Knowing his way through the fortress, Djedar made his way down the corridor until he stopped before a heavy wooden door, kicking it open. The heat of the moment and desperation of escape let him ignore the pain jolting up his leg from the strength of the lock, the same way it had let him push past the persistent aching in his spine since the night of the monster attack.

Tefnahkt's chambers were almost more lavish than his main hall, but they had no time to admire the tapestries along the walls or the enormous bed of crimson and red taking up one side of the room. Djedar motioned everyone inside, shutting the door behind them and dropping over it a heavy bar that Tefnahkt had ready and waiting.

"His private chambers?" said Buharum, giving a low whistle. "Didn't think a man as ugly as Tefnahkt could entertain women, but his bed's big enough for three... or four..."

"Jokes even *now*, Buharum?" Farrah snapped, her voice quivering. Djedar couldn't tell if it was from rage, sorrow, or both.

"Tefnahkt," said Djedar, "born in Kemhet but calling the empire of Parsanshar his home, admired a custom popular among many of that land's kings and priests of old..."

The barred door jolted, making most of them start, but not Djedar. He took hold of a bronze sconce beside Tefnahkt's bed, gripping it firmly and twisting it sideways until a harsh thud sounded through the room. Again someone slammed into the barricade. Guards barked orders and heavy footfalls ran up and down the corridor outside, probably bringing something with which to ram the door.

But their escape route made itself plain. A nearby portion of the wall decorated in a depiction of the mighty serpent Apophis fell inward and slid aside. A dark passage awaited them, seemingly reminiscent of the path Apophis himself took each night.

"I'll lead," said Djedar. "Keep up, but watch your step. There are a lot of stairs, and we don't have any light."

"How do you know this passage?" asked Dunewalker.

"I helped build it," Djedar answered simply. "I've been Tefnahkt's slave for many years."

They plunged into the dark passage. Djedar felt along the walkways and stairs that seemed as familiar as the day he helped construct the palace. He hadn't designed the mechanisms of the escape route, but he had watched those who did, while doing his own hard labor: bringing them the stones of the fortress itself. Engineers and architects watched and told them what to do, all the while thinking him an inattentive fool.

Steadily, they picked up speed. Far behind them, they heard the crash of the barricaded door as the guards spilled into Tefnahkt's quarters, and Djedar sped up, going as fast as he could without losing his footing and tripping down one of the treacherous stairs. This passage let them sneak through the very guts of the fortress, moving through its thick stone walls from the inside – walls which outside observers would think perfectly solid.

"I'm surprised Tefnahkt didn't just – kill us all while he could," Buharum remarked between breaths as he sprinted to keep up with the tall folk.

"As a demon-worshiper, his power is limited," Dunewalker said. "What he used on Solon kept him from easily killing the rest of us. His magic comes from his soulstones that fuels his pact with a demon... or else his own soul. He is not a true mage, like those so rarely gifted magic at birth."

"He wants some in reserve in case we catch up with him at the tomb," Farrah added grimly. "And maybe to get into it in the first place..."

"Yes. It's almost the new moon. If we can't follow him now, we'll never catch him in time."

A light reached Djedar's eyes from cracks in a hidden door up ahead, and he set off at a run, prompting the others to do the same. "We'll catch him," said Djedar. "We can't let the Wastes trick our minds like it did before – it's not that far from here to the dig site. Not as far as it seemed when my convoy got lost."

"*My* mind will not be tricked," promised Dunewalker.

Running his fingers along the stones beside the hidden door, Djedar found a loose one and depressed it. Immediately, the door started sliding aside. Cool morning air wafted into the stuffy escape passage, but

Djedar squeezed himself through before the door even finished opening, stumbling out into the streets of Tefnahkt's walled town once more.

They were behind the fortress. He took barely a moment to orient himself before he spun left, speeding up again. They had to reach the stables before someone else did – and before the guards came down upon them from behind. Hopefully, navigating Tefnahkt's escape route was proving difficult for them... but even so, there would be others searching outside.

"Slow down!" Buharum shouted. "You're losing us, Rath!"

"Don't tell him to wait!" Dunewalker barked. "There's no time; we can catch up!"

"The stables!" Djedar called over his shoulder. "We have to reach the gates before they bar us inside!"

He didn't wait. It didn't take him long to burst through the already-open stable side door, and he found all the animals there as they'd left them – save for one horse. Tefnahkt must have taken it. But the Medjai horses remained, as did the falcon...

And the elephant.

Behind him, the Medjai stumbled one by one into the stables, the two dwarves panting from exertion. "And how," said Buharum despite being so winded, "do you plan to get through those closed gates?"

A wicked smile pulled at Djedar's lips as he approached the elephant, reaching out a hand once more. The elephant lifted its trunk to touch his hand, slowly flapping its huge ears.

"No gates are closed for *you*, are they, my friend?" Djedar said, looking into the elephant's weary eyes. "Let's find freedom together, shall we?"

The Medjai needed no orders, assembling around their horses. Dunewalker helped Farrah haul Solon onto her steed before mounting his own, while Buharum and Kukrum mounted the horse they shared. Djedar fetched some more cloth from nearby to wrap around his arms, throwing a bag of falcon bait over his shoulder and enlisting the aid of the Medjai to quickly suit up the elephant in some supplies and a saddle. All it took after that was a soft murmured command to the elephant for the great beast to bow and let Djedar climb up onto its back.

Once in place, he looked back at the Medjai on their horses. Dunewalker seemed impressed, while Farrah only worried about the still-unconscious Solon – and Buharum and Kukrum both stared up at him in disbelief, the latter's expression bordering on outrage.

Djedar said, "No matter what happens, you stay behind me."

Dunewalker nodded. "We will follow you, Rath."

Vigor filled him. His wicked smile from before returned, and it was all Djedar could do to fight a full grin as he set the elephant off. It moved at a seemingly leisurely pace toward the tallest doors on the stable, still open from Tefnahkt's escape.

Atop the elephant, Djedar saw everything. The squat buildings of Tefnahkt's town almost matched the height as the animal he rode upon, with only the fortress towering notably higher. Every street around them seemed empty, but a clamor gathered in the distance toward the main gates.

The elephant continued its calm pace, covering more ground than a man at a quick jog. It carried Djedar out into the main street, where he saw the gates of the town's outer walls—

Like he suspected, the guards already worked to close them. But those gates were only wood, with no metal portcullis as reinforcement – and they weren't closed yet.

Djedar sat up, giving a sharp whistle and pulling a piece of bait from the bag. The falcon flew from the stables, landing on Djedar's outstretched hand to accept his offering of a scrap.

"Lead me to your master," Djedar whispered to it. "Find Tefnahkt. I know you can."

And he let it fly, watching the raptor soar over the walls and out into the Wastes. It would find Tefnahkt – and it would lead them straight to him… or, if nothing else, straight back to the dig site of Ankhu's tomb.

Now to get out of the walls.

"Yahura!" he ordered his mount. *"Imshi!"*

Djedar braced himself against the elephant's back as it picked up speed. He dared not look behind him and make sure Dunewalker and the other Medjai were still in tow – he just had to hope they were keeping up. He could only focus on the gates dead ahead.

"This'll never work!" came a shriek – Kukrum, sounding terrified.

"Just stay *behind* me!" Dunewalker commanded in a powerful bellow.

Wind rushed in Djedar's ears. Exhilaration made his heart race like never before. The elephant scarcely seemed to walk quickly at first, but suddenly it broke into a steady saunter. Though it didn't gallop like a horse, its long, steady gait would strike harder than a battering ram. Guards in the streets ahead scattered as the elephant charged, helpless to stop it.

The gates were almost shut, with only a sliver of pale morning light diffused in the unnatural fog of the Wastes peeking between the two tremendous doors – but the elephant didn't stop. Djedar braced himself, ducking his head low and covering his skull with one arm while holding on for dear life.

The elephant met the gates head-on. Impact rattled him to the bone. The animal didn't even slow, knocking one gate right off its hinges and sending splinters into the sand. The other gate slammed into the opposite side of the wall, barely holding on but still splitting apart where the elephant's tusks had struck it.

That mighty beast made it all seem so effortless as it burst through the fortress gates and out into the emptiness of the cursed desert. Onward the elephant ran into the light, lifting its trunk as if in triumph and trumpeting a call into the desolation.

The grin Djedar had staved off before spread over his face. He sat up again, patting the elephant's tough hide. "Excellent work, my friend," he said with a laugh. "We made it."

Even knowing it was far from over, this felt closer than he'd ever come to being free of Tefnahkt – closer still than the last time he thought he'd managed to escape...

But Tefnahkt's men weren't done yet.

Though they passed into the Wastes, voices still cried out at their backs. Djedar watched as the Medjai on their horses arrived on either side of the elephant, riding alongside him.

"Archers on the walls!" called Kukrum. "Watch yourselves!"

"Take them out!" answered Farrah. Dunewalker drew a long spear from a quiver of javelins on his horse's saddle, and Buharum reached for his crossbow. Feeling suddenly helpless, Djedar could only lean low over the elephant and hope arrows didn't rain down upon them—

"Riders!" Dunewalker shouted next.

Slave-drivers and guards and even some armed slaves from Tefnahkt's fortress galloped at all speed. Spears raised, they made to intercept them. Farrah urged her horse forward, trying to keep the limp Solon from falling out of the saddle – and taking her place beside Djedar's elephant was not one but two enemy riders. They raised spears and made to attack the elephant's legs.

But the mighty beast swung toward them, tilting its head their way and slamming the full weight of its massive form into their horses. It caught one rider on its tusk and sent him, screaming and flailing, into the sand. The other went down steed and rider alike, bowled over by the elephant's weight. An arrow whistled past Djedar's ear from the archers far at their backs, and he ducked again with a quick swear to Horus.

Still more riders came up around them— and then something else appeared.

Blemmyes. The headless men. Like spectres of another world, their distorted forms emerged from the sands on either side of the scarcely carved path through the dunes that led into the Tefnahkt's fortress. Djedar went cold with fear. How did they even *see* from such a hiding place? Or had they been invisible, using some dark magic?

It didn't matter. They had them surrounded. All of them.

But the headless men bellowed and lifted javelins, throwing them at the enemy horsemen with all the expertise of Kemhet's greatest warriors. Others raised bows, loosing up at the archers on the walls. Still more appeared seemingly from the desert itself as if one with the very sand, rushing from the Wastes and racing past the elephant and the horses, straight toward the broken gates.

The headless abominations ignored the Medjai, focusing only on Tefnahkt's town and keep. Djedar lifted himself and stared in wide-eyed confusion, watching the blemmyes launch a full-scale attack now that the fortress was compromised. Terrified guards were forced back, away from Djedar and the others –

back to their walls, in hopes of making a stand against the headless creatures.

Though Djedar slowed the elephant and his companions did the same for their horses, they didn't stop. Still, he had to witness the blemmyes begin their charge now that they had an opening. They were ruthless, painting their distorted bodies in the blood of the slain slave-drivers – those who had hunted their kind.

"The blemmyes!" shouted Kukrum, his voice cracking. "They're – they're helping us!?"

"I'm not sure they *meant* to," answered Farrah. "They're after Tefnahkt."

"They're after his fortress," added Dunewalker, looking behind them even as they kept riding.

But Djedar frowned and cast a glance over to Solon where he rested in Farrah's saddle, his flesh burnt and twisted, still without consciousness and barely breathing.

Djedar finally let himself relax, patting the elephant beneath him again. "Or maybe Solon was right... the gods *did* put them here for a reason."

Maybe, he had to think – just maybe, they weren't alone on this mission after all.

The ride through the Wastes felt like a dream, as though their great journey from before had been a falsehood. Though the Blasted Wastes were unimaginably vast, so too could they play tricks on the mind – and one could get lost easily. Even with a map, Buharum knew he couldn't say where Tefnahkt had put his hidden fortress. Nothing about the Wastes could be precise.

But with a clear path and Djedar seeming to know exactly where to go, they halted only occasionally to give the animals a brief respite. Now and then, the falcon from Tefnahkt's stables reappeared to receive a scrap of meat from Djedar – and then it would fly off again, and Djedar would have them follow it.

"We're following a *bird?*" Buharum asked at one point.

"He will lead us true," Djedar answered.

Buharum frowned, unsure. "You favor Horus, don't you, Kemheti?"

Djedar snorted. "I'm glad you noticed."

"I figured you must. That's why you'll put your life in the talons of a falcon."

"I trust Horus's judgment... as I trust the judgment of Anubis."

Buharum spoke his next words before he let himself think. "But you also fear it. Don't you?"

Djedar paused. Buharum had seen it in Djedar's eyes, back in Tefnahkt's fortress – the fear of death. He'd seen it countless times before in the eyes of almost every Man as well as some of his fellow Besak-ha when in battle, but he hadn't expected to see it so strongly in the eyes of this stone-hearted slave. To his credit, Djedar hadn't abandoned them yet, but Buharum was beginning to wonder... How much trust could they put in a slave who hungered so much for freedom and feared for his life?

A Medjai wasn't meant to fear for his life, at least never to the point of putting it before the mission. A Medjai knew his life wasn't what mattered, and he would give it for something greater – like Solon. Kukrum hadn't been entirely wrong about that.

Buharum's question earned him only a glance from Djedar, a side-eye cutting his way for half a second. Buharum stared at Djedar all the while, waiting for an answer, but he didn't get one. The former slave kept his eyes straight ahead, setting his jaw.

Dunewalker spoke instead, saying quietly, "So do we all."

Farrah scarcely said a word for the entire journey. Each rest, they checked on Solon – and nothing changed. He still breathed, but it was shallow and weak. His marred skin made him barely look like himself. He seemed to have no tattoos left in several places on his body, as if they had been blasted out from his very flesh to leave it twisted and hideously scarred. From the look on Dunewalker's face every time he checked on him, Buharum knew it was a miracle that Solon still held onto life at all.

Then, at long last, they finally left behind the Blasted Wastes. They still had to travel through the red sands of Deshret before they would reach the dig site of Ankhu's tomb once more, but for now, they stopped again – and Farrah turned her horse to face them.

"I can't go there," she said. "I can't take Solon to that place. He's barely made it through the Wastes. I'm taking him to the nearest Medjai outpost."

"You can't go alone," Buharum declared.

Farrah shook her head. "Deshret is my home – I know where to go, I know where the Medjai fortresses are. I *have* to get Solon help— there *has* to be some way to save him."

"There is," said Dunewalker. "Go, Farrah. I wish I could come with you, but we cannot let Tefnahkt open the tomb."

"The new moon arrives in two nights, and then Ankhu will rise again to wander his labyrinth," added

Kukrum. "We'll have to make it to the dig site before then – if we even *can*."

"Go," ordered Farrah – but Djedar's elephant bowed, letting him slide down from his perch.

"Farrah, wait," he said. "Take him," he motioned back to the elephant. "He'll get you through the desert and keep you safe."

Farrah blinked, staring in wordless surprise, looking between Djedar and the elephant with no idea what to say. But Dunewalker dismounted to help Djedar get Solon off Farrah's horse and move him to the elephant instead, which again remained bowed as they did their work.

Once Farrah climbed up the elephant, Djedar rubbed the animal's trunk and spoke a few gentle words. It straightened again and leaned subtly in his direction. Buharum scoffed and shook his head despite a smile trying to find his lips.

"A slave and his elephant," Buharum remarked quietly.

"Shh, brother," Kukrum chided, "he'll hear you."

"Kill him for me," said Farrah, watching from atop the elephant. "Kill Tefnahkt for what he did to Solon."

Dunewalker nodded. "We will, Farrah."

"Swear it," Farrah ordered, each word dripping with a thirst for blood. Dunewalker set his jaw, but before

Buharum or Kukrum could speak, Djedar mounted the horse which had been Farrah's and regarded her solemnly.

"*I* swear it," he said firmly.

"Just want to be sure no one takes pity on him," Farrah said. "Especially not you, Kukrum, with all your kindness... although you weren't ready to spare any for Solon."

Kukrum clammed up, and no one said any more.

Thus, they parted ways. Farrah rode the elephant off into the rolling red land of Deshret, while Buharum swung his horse around to rejoin Djedar and Dunewalker. They resumed following the falcon toward the distant dig site of Ankhu's tomb. Behind Buharum, Kukrum shifted in the saddle, obviously uncomfortable.

"The greater good isn't always what Men would call kind," Kukrum muttered under his breath.

"Don't keep pushing it," Buharum advised. The others didn't hear them, thankfully, striking up discussion of their own.

"I'm not sure two nights is enough time to reach the tomb," said Dunewalker.

Djedar nodded. "Tefnahkt will push his horse for all speed. He doesn't care if it dies by the time he reaches the tomb again; he just wants to make sure he's there for Ankhu's awakening."

"I love horses, and I love *my* horse, but I'd prefer an exhausted horse over a risen godlike nightmare destroying three or more lands," Buharum remarked.

There was no mirth in his words, for he meant every one of them. The three Medjai and the escaped slave hastened their steeds, with no time to waste. Even now, Tefnahkt neared the tomb. He would find a way inside even if he had to blast one himself with his power, and the new moon would awaken the mummy within.

They couldn't let that happen. Tefnahkt could not open the tomb and free Ankhu – no matter the cost.

PART II

The sun, steadily reddening, started sinking low toward the horizon by the time they reached the dig site where the slaves worked tirelessly to uncover the Tomb of Ankhu. That didn't give them much time – not much at all.

Since they had left the dig site but a few days ago, much had changed. Instead of working tirelessly on digging out almost innumerable chambers to uncover the long-buried labyrinthine tomb from the sands, the slaves were now gathered in hordes near the center of the dig site. Slave-drivers patrolled around them but looked only half-hearted, their attention elsewhere. Smaller groups of slaves were scattered here and there amidst the dunes and sands and statues, but all of them had their faces flat against the ground in prayer regardless of where they were. While the Kemheti gods were not generally worshiped in such a way, Tefnahkt, like Ankhu, made demands of his followers to scrape and bow.

Lord Tefnahkt the Red must have passed this way very recently. Only his presence could have left them in such reverence. It was not the many statues of the animal-headed Kemheti gods – particularly the mighty wolf-headed Anubis, whose presence seemed inescapable on the walls and across the many standing or resting statues outside the tomb – that had the slaves in such wonder.

Buharum slowed his steed and looked to the heavens, watching as the falcon they had followed through the desert swooped down to land once more on the outstretched hand of Djedar Rath. Buharum still thought Djedar's own features, with his deep-set eyes shadowed by his dark brow and beak-like nose, strangely favored the bird of prey that he fed a scrap of meat.

"Can't believe a bird led us all the way through the desert," Buharum said. Behind him in the shared saddle, Kukrum grunted in agreement.

Djedar cut his dark eyes Buharum's way briefly, a small smile playing on his lips. "You can always trust a well-treated animal."

"You seem to have a talent for them." Buharum snorted. "More than you do with people, honestly."

Dunewalker ran a hand over his smooth, ebon-skinned head. "Right now, I trust only my fellow Medjai. When the sun sets tonight, Ankhu will find an open door: something he hasn't seen for thousands of years."

"I don't care to see a walking mummy – I'll leave those for the stories," Buharum remarked. "Think we can reach Tefnahkt before he sets that creature free?"

"We only have a few hours."

"It'll be enough," said Djedar, though he appeared to be speaking to the falcon still resting on his cloth-wrapped arm. "We've come this far. We can't approach the tomb like this, though. Follow me."

Buharum had learned not to ask questions; Djedar generally wouldn't answer them or would give some kind of irreverent joke. He simply turned his horse to trail after the former slave's steed once again. Djedar led them toward a far outer side of the dig site, releasing the falcon before dismounting his horse and waiting for everyone else to follow. Kukrum climbed down the short ladder on the saddle of their horse, and Buharum followed shortly after him. Dunewalker hitched the horses on some nearby posts – and paused as he saw another horse already there.

"This one," he said, "was in the stables at Tefnahkt's fortress when we first arrived there."

Djedar intoned a low, dark hum in thought, but that was all. Buharum frowned; the only person to leave that fortress before them had been Lord Tefnahkt himself. Which meant he was definitely here, as if the slaves' behavior hadn't clued them in enough.

With that, Djedar resumed leading the way. Clad as he was only in a *shendyt*, essentially a long white loincloth, and little else other than his deep olive skin, Djedar blended in with the slaves. But with his lanky, muscular build, he looked far more vicious than most – particularly thanks to the black-bladed crescent *khopesh* sword hanging at his hip. None of the other slaves carried weapons of any sort.

The rest of the group stood out even worse, so it surprised Buharum when no one seemed to care about their passage. Even as they neared the dig site itself, the slaves ignored them, remaining on their knees... though they seemed to be facing random directions, having dropped into their position of worship on the spot.

Again Buharum stroked the enormous beard tucked into his belt. If the slaves weren't facing the entrance to the tomb, how were they supposed to find it in such a massive dig site of confusing passageways and blocked-off excavation sites?

Most of the slaves they passed muttered under their breaths. Buharum didn't understand all the words; it didn't sound like they were speaking Kemheti. He cast a quick look back at Dunewalker in an unasked question: what were these people saying?

Dunewalker, his brow furrowed, returned the look and said quietly, "Demon-worshipers... Using demonic tongue. I don't think even *they* know what they are saying, but they speak of sacrificing the souls of the unworthy to further Tefnahkt's power – and the return of Ankhu."

"Well, that's gonna happen if we can't find the entrance in a hurry," Buharum muttered.

"Every doorway leads nowhere," Dunewalker said, pointing to one as they passed. "How many false entrances did the gods put here?"

"Dozens," Djedar answered.

Onward they walked. No slave budged at their passage, and Djedar carefully steered them away from the few patrolling slave-drivers. Buharum couldn't help but note the skill with which Djedar avoided his masters, stalking in and out amidst the statues and uncovered entrances in the deep dig site, staying close to the shadows.

Until, at last, his patience broke. In the middle of their search, Djedar suddenly lunged for a nearby slave, grabbed the skinny, shorter man by the one long braid at the back of his head, and hauled him up to his feet. The slave yelped but barely resisted, going stiff and letting himself be lifted. Djedar pulled his head back and glared.

"Where is he?" Djedar snarled in the slave's face. Not loudly, not angrily, but with a kind of false calm that betrayed scarcely-contained violence.

The slave's eyes snapped open and stared into Djedar's. He started to squirm and said, "Lord Tefnahkt the Red, summoner of the Pharaoh Ankhu—"

"Skip his damned titles and tell me where he is. Where's the entrance to the tomb?"

The slave put on a maddened grin. "He goes to fulfill his destiny. He will become one with..."

Djedar backhanded the other slave across the jaw so hard the man's head snapped to one side. Buharum winced at the meaty impact that sounded harder than a punch.

"Tell me," Djedar ordered, his deep voice even lower now, each word a smooth and clear threat. "You know I'll do what I must."

"Rath," Dunewalker snapped, stepping forward and putting a heavy hand on Djedar's shoulder, "this isn't how we get our answers."

Buharum merely stood by, watching. The slave was so far beyond their help, so lost in his belief that the cultist Tefnahkt was some kind of god, would it really matter if Djedar *did* break the man's neck? This man and his ilk would watch gleefully while Tefnahkt slaughtered thousands, if he could. It was sad, yes, but it was true.

Beside him, Kukrum looked horrified. Even after all they had witnessed, and even after managing to liberate one slave, Kukrum still seemed to want to save them all – including the people who drove those slaves. *Ridiculous*, Buharum thought. But Kukrum was, after all, the nice one.

But the slave's emaciated face twisted into a smile, and he started laughing. He didn't seem capable of stopping, either. Djedar threw him to the ground, leaving him there cackling and curling into a fetal position. Then Djedar pulled away from Dunewalker's hand and kept walking.

"These people sold their souls a long time ago," Djedar said. "What good ones were left have either escaped or died trying. I know, because I saw it happen. Tefnahkt 'purified' his servants of all doubt against him."

"You mentioned you had felt his magic," Dunewalker said, his words slow and cautious. "Did he...?"

Dunewalker let his question drift. Buharum wasn't sure this was the time or place, finding their way across the dig site with the sun ever closer to setting. Every grain of sand in the hourglass currently worked toward Tefnahkt's victory.

"He tortured me," Djedar finally answered. "The other slaves were made to watch. They laughed and called me a traitor. No one tried to stop him. No one even spared a shred of remorse – or a drop to drink when it was all over." Djedar kept his eyes forward, but Buharum could see the tension rise in his shoulders, the memories alone clearly angering him. "Tefnahkt kept me for sport. I never gave up, and that amused him. I alone survived while everyone else who dared defy him died to his dark arts."

"Your soul must be exceptionally strong."

Djedar scoffed. "I've heard that one before."

"So you'll make it his mistake, letting you live so long," Kukrum guessed.

"Yes," Djedar replied firmly. "I will."

Finally, they found their goal. Someone must have dispersed the slaves they'd seen from afar, as only a few of them remained, still on their knees with their heads bowed low and their eyes closed in reverence. Slave-drivers patrolled here thicker than anywhere else – no way they could get close without being spotted.

It was not a grand thing. Statues of Anubis stood on either side of an otherwise unremarkable entranceway that had once been buried in the sand. Judging by the condition of the area, Tefnahkt had blasted his way through what had once been a sturdy stone door or even a false wall and entered the tomb from there. So they had been correct in their assumption: the reason Tefnahkt hadn't simply used his power to kill them all before was to save his energy for blasting his way into the tomb... and to drive back anyone who would stop him.

Buharum still didn't savor the idea of doing battle with that warlock, especially after what he'd done to Solon.

Djedar halted at the base of a yet another great statue of Anubis, staying in the hard shadows of the bright sunset. He looked back at the others while Dunewalker moved forward, assessing the situation.

"The slaves will help their masters," said Dunewalker. "If we attack, we'll be overwhelmed."

"And the slave-drivers are guarding the entrance," Kukrum pointed out, nodding toward the group of four men who stood around the open doorway, weapons at the ready. "I'm sure Tefnahkt told them to keep an eye out for us."

Buharum cursed and said, "We don't have a *choice*. We can't let Ankhu out, and the bastard's going to rise in a few hours to look for his heart—"

"Don't panic. We can't get reckless *now*, brother," Kukrum chided, and Buharum scowled at him.

"You don't have to be," said Djedar. "I've got an idea. Stay here – you'll know when to move."

Before Buharum could ask what the plan was, Djedar left, slipping into the shadows behind them and then seeming to disappear altogether. Buharum threw his hands in the air, and Kukrum patted him on the shoulder.

"What're we supposed to do, move on his mark? How're we supposed to pick him out among all the others?"

"Well, just look for his hair," Kukrum replied with an encouraging smile. "Most of the slaves have none. And his sword on his hip. And his big ears."

Dunewalker snorted, though there wasn't much mirth in it. "I don't think it's *him* he'll want us to see."

If there was one thing that could wake the slaves and the masters from their stupor, it was the treasure room.

Over the course of the dig site's existence, one of the earliest finds of interest had been dubbed the 'treasure room' by the slave-drivers. Hieroglyphs along the edges of the room warned to stay away, that the gold was cursed. Its finders, of course, had ignored those warnings in favor of something else: the massive mountain of wealth on the far side of the chamber.

That gold, however, lay behind a wall of bars no man knew how to penetrate. They too were golden in color, but they were clearly of some other metal – they were sturdier than anything any of them had ever encountered. No matter how hard someone hit it, the bars didn't budge nor even seem dented. Perhaps they too were cursed. Djedar didn't know. Before, he'd scarcely paid attention to talk of this room.

Of other importance in the chamber was the fact that its support pillars stood only tenuously. The slave-drivers had warned the diggers that the entire room could collapse at any moment. One pillar was particularly concerning, worn as it was. Thus, Lord Tefnahkt the Red had given explicit orders to all slave-drivers to keep the slaves out of the chamber entirely until they could discover how to reach the treasure behind the bars. He didn't want to risk losing access to so many riches.

Too bad, Djedar thought as he made his way across the dig site. The Medjai whom he traveled here with had thankfully remained behind as he'd instructed. This left him alone to do as he pleased without observation.

He knew the location of the treasure chamber very well, after years of having to navigate around it while receiving death glares from its guardians. Now, however, as he approached the tall doorway which seemed to reach outward from the side of a great sand dune, Djedar found the chamber unattended. Even so much gold seemed like nothing in the face of finally freeing the ancient Pharaoh Ankhu the Endless.

Giving one last cursory glance at his surroundings to make sure no one would catch him, Djedar approached the yawning square entrance. It rested under a set of colorful hieroglyphics warning of certain doom to those who would dare touch the riches within, but Djedar simply strode into the treasure chamber.

Here, under the watchful gaze of many animal-headed depictions of his gods carved and painted into the walls, Djedar found a room of sandstone alight with torches the slave-drivers kept burning. A statue of his favored deity Horus watched from the far end of the room, his eyes sapphires lined with gold, set into a falcon head painted white and blue. He stretched out partially from the walls and partially from the ceiling, his entire front and arms reaching out over a glimmering trove of gold and jewels like nothing Djedar figured would ever see again.

Goblets, plates, scepters, crooks, tall crowns, bangles, anklets, pectorals... endless mountains of treasure ranging from jewelry to eating utensils to stacks of coins like the hoard of a dragon rested beyond the golden bars. A gilded cage for gilded riches.

Yet all those riches didn't tempt Djedar. It didn't take the stare of Horus to deter him; he simply thought nothing of it. Perhaps, he thought, always having nothing affected him differently than it did some of the other slaves, who had occasionally tried to steal into the chamber and see if they could reach even a single coin beyond the bars.

Two massive columns of stone reached up the middle of the room. Others stood beyond the barrier, but the only one that mattered was to Djedar's left, almost entirely worn away. The stones holding it together had become chipped and thinned, though Djedar couldn't say how.

Several tools remained scattered about the room, ones the slave-drivers had used to assault the bars separating them from the hoard. Djedar quickly found a heavy sledgehammer and hefted it from its place against the wall. He tested the weight of it, then approached the unstable pillar – and swung with all his might.

His first blow shook everything, knocking dust from the ceiling and sand from between cracks in the stones forming the chamber. It also shook *him*, sending a shock of pain shooting up his arms and especially into his back, which hadn't ever gotten much of a chance to heal or even rest. Djedar cringed at the pain but braced himself and swung again.

It hurt worse this time – but the pillar shuddered from his blow. An ominous crack split the stillness of the room. Then another. And another—

But Djedar lifted the hammer one more time and hit it again, right at its weakest point. The pillar cracked visibly, a black line starting to reach up its middle. Another webbed out from the first...

Djedar dropped the hammer and ran.

Dust rained from the ceiling as the room shook. He didn't look behind him to watch the pillar break and collapse. Sand filling the already close air choked him as he bolted for the exit, almost tripping over a pickaxe someone had left in the floor.

Stumbling, he threw himself out the doorway. A deafening crash like thunder resounded right behind him, spitting sand all over his back and head – and running a quick chill up his spine at how easily he could've crushed himself.

Voices erupted across the camp. Djedar scrambled to his feet, making for the nearest shadows as the spell over the dig site broke. Footsteps rushed toward the sound of the collapsing chamber, slaves and slave-drivers alike hurrying to see – and Djedar took a long way around back to where he'd left his Medjai companions waiting.

Only they weren't waiting. Djedar returned to the entrance of Ankhu's tomb to find Dunewalker, sword in hand, standing over a dispatched slave-driver who lay spread-eagled at his feet. Behind him, Buharum checked a second slave-driver with his boot, giving him a good shove – the man had a crossbow bolt in his leg and another in his chest. He didn't move.

Dunewalker looked impressed. "Good work," he said. "Whatever you did, it concerned them. Nearly all of them went to the noise."

"I buried what Tefnahkt wanted almost as much as he wanted Ankhu himself," Djedar replied.

"Let me guess," said Buharum, "gold?"

"Of course."

The dwarf scoffed. "Men and their gold..."

Dunewalker gave a laugh. "And the *Besak-ha* are known for their generosity, are they?"

Kukrum offered a sly smile. "He has us there, brother. Though we're far more generous than our northern brethren, or so I hear."

"Certainly being generous with our lives," Buharum muttered.

The entrance to Ankhu's tomb wasn't as impressive visually as Djedar imagined – yet he knew the gods had tried to keep it inconspicuous. They had succeeded. If he hadn't known what it was, he would've believed it to be any of the countless false entrances they'd found over the course of the dig site's long existence.

Hieroglyphs inscribed around the square doorway, their colors partially worn away by sand and the endless march of time, warned of an ancient curse. A pair of wolf-headed Anubis statues guarded either side of the door, staring straight ahead, their own colors worn away so starkly that they looked like simple sandstone: a far cry from the black and gold, colorful statues of the same make Djedar had seen in cities. If a door or gate had ever stood under the tall frame over the statues' heads, Tefnahkt had blasted it to pieces with his magic.

And yet something about this doorway, about the yawning void awaiting within, sent a chill into Djedar's very soul. This wasn't at all like the walls pretending to be doors or the empty dead-end chambers they had discovered. The darkness waiting ahead of them held so much energy, so much raw *power*, that Djedar felt certain he could feel it in his very skin.

No, not only power... Evil. An evil so terrible something in his body physically recoiled at its presence.

Dunewalker clearly felt it, too, from the way he paused and stared wide-eyed into the darkness for a moment. But he soon turned to one of the two torches the slave-drivers had left burning on either side of the doorway, pulling one off its mount. Djedar took the other.

But when he looked into the shadows again, fear bit hard at the back of his neck. Why would he enter such a cursed place – literally and truly cursed and so full of evil it made his stomach tie itself into knots? Why shouldn't he just escape and take his victory at long last?

Hadn't he spent a hard enough life already, struggled enough to achieve even the briefest taste of freedom? What loyalty did he even have to these Medjai and their ancient order? Except... would his freedom matter, or even last, if Ankhu truly rose and reshaped all of Kemhet in his own evil image?

Dunewalker strode forward into the tomb. Kukrum followed him – and Buharum paused, looking back at Djedar, a hard scowl etched into his stern, heavy, dwarven features. He looked as though he expected Djedar to turn tail and run.

And why *shouldn't* he?

But – he didn't.

His hesitation concluded, Djedar tightened his grip on the burning torch in his hand, while he drew in his other his recently-acquired black-bladed sword. Then he plunged into the tomb, picking up the pace to join Dunewalker at the head of the group.

A heartbeat.

Almost the very moment one of his feet crossed the threshold of that tomb, Djedar heard it. A deep, steady rhythm haunted the narrow corridor, coming from all around him, echoing against every stone – the endless beating of a heart...

Ankhu the Endless's cursed, eternal heart.

The gods truly *had* cursed him to always hear what he sought most. The sound made Djedar hesitate again. He stopped in his tracks, hands sweating. He watched the light from Dunewalker's torch ahead spread out into a large chamber which awaited him, but the sound of the heart turned his blood to ice.

At length, however, he did join Dunewalker and the two dwarves in the room awaiting them down the long stone hallway. Even more statues of Anubis and only a select few depictions of other gods lined the walls and stood watch around the pillars holding up the chamber.

But the room was empty. Djedar lifted his torch in search of anything interesting, but all he found were some shattered canopic jars: containers for the important organs of the mummified dead. Each one was topped always by the head of a different deity who watched over certain organs. But the contents of these jars were missing. They looked ancient...

And there were dozens of them. They hid in corners around the room, littered the floor, all of them broken.

"Tricks," Buharum said. "I'll bet these jars came from all around the tomb. Ankhu was looking for his heart – makes sense he'd search a canopic jar."

"But hearts are never meant to be removed," Djedar muttered almost to himself. "They're certainly not meant for jars..."

"That's how the gods denied him passage to the afterlife," said Dunewalker. "That is why he searches for it whenever he rises on the new moon, trapped in his tomb, as Solon said. If he found his heart, perhaps he could finally find peace, or else total destruction of his soul. Either way, it would be an end to his suffering."

"And he has to *listen* to it," Kukrum added with a shudder. "They really were trying to torment him, weren't they?"

Djedar's gaze roamed over the many hieroglyphs and other pictures along the walls. He saw some familiar concepts, namely the same pharaoh from before. He rode a golden chariot on one wall, and on another, the gods subdued him and took him away in those black chains – Djedar had seen those images before, elsewhere in the dig site.

"Makes you wonder what exactly he did," Djedar commented grimly. "It must've been awful, to get the gods' own attention. They only ever watch us, at least usually... it's not like they descend and punish every evildoer. Why handle him so personally?" He looked at the Medjai for answers – surely they, and their ancient order, knew still more than what they had told him. "Who *was* Ankhu – or *what* was he?"

Buharum shrugged, still looking around the chamber like everyone else. "Important to the gods, apparently. That's all we know."

"Some say his atrocities were so great the gods *had* to step in," said Kukrum. "It was a very exceptional case."

"And yet they never stepped in for other tyrants, not even ones summoning demons to our world," Djedar replied. "Not even the most unstoppable ones – like Ildrius in Achaea."

Kukrum quirked a bushy brow. "A slave who knows even foreign history? Er – pardon me, I mean no offense. I'm just surprised."

Djedar snorted. "None taken."

"I've heard comparisons of Ankhu and Ildrius," Buharum commented. "Both extremely powerful, both using magic to bend everything to their will... but Ankhu was different. I don't know how; I just know he was."

Djedar lifted his head. "Even the Medjai don't know, then?"

"No," answered Dunewalker, speaking at last.

He stood before the far wall, looking at something depicted there, holding his torch toward it. Djedar joined him – and saw the same pharaoh so often depicted, but now with a skull-like face and his body covered in the wrappings of a mummy, holding a man by the throat. The mummy Pharaoh Ankhu's maw was open wide, and flowing into it was a golden light from the man he restrained.

Buharum joined them, his face pale. "Surely he's not like those soul-eaters, those things cursed at birth. They can actually rip someone's soul out and just... swallow it. Nothing else can do that, I thought. Except... maybe demons themselves."

"And I thought it was *people* cursed like that, not 'things,'" Kukrum remarked.

Buharum stroked his beard again but said nothing, fear written deep in his swarthy face.

"Let us hope Ankhu does not also possess that power," said Dunewalker, grimmer than ever.

Of all the passages leading from the chamber, they found only one that wasn't a dead end. They regrouped there before setting off. Djedar had never considered himself claustrophobic, but the narrow halls and choking lack of air in Ankhu's tomb still managed to shred his nerves... or perhaps it was the close quarters combined with the endless, slow beating of the heart.

It never stopped. Never slowed. And everywhere they went, he could still hear it, throbbing in his own ears as if it was a part of him.

The sound wasn't affecting only him, either. Buharum's every muscle looked ready to snap under his sturdy armor, his eyes wide and white as he kept looking over his shoulder, throwing Djedar glances, and checking to make sure his clan-brother Kukrum still trailed close behind them. Kukrum himself white-knuckle clutched his crescent axe, which matched Buharum's own. Dunewalker didn't make a sound, his jaw set so hard the tension was visible on the sides of his perfectly shaven face.

Torchlight danced off colored hieroglyphs along the walls. They depicted scenes of torment and torture, people suffering in droves under plagues of insects and shadow. Shades of white, red, green, blue, and even gold lined the walls, vividly telling tales of horror and suffering – the tales of Ankhu's reign.

But many of the hieroglyphs had been angrily marred by... "Are those – claw marks?" Buharum asked, almost choking between words.

No one answered, at least not in words. Several grave looks were exchanged among the lot of them.

"*Men* don't have claws," Kukrum murmured, his voice low. "So *mummies* shouldn't have claws... they're just man corpses. It isn't possible, is it?"

"Mummies also are not meant to walk," said Djedar.

In the haunting torchlight, Djedar noticed something else. Holes dotted the walls all around them, intentionally and perfectly placed amidst the carven stones. He stopped long enough to carefully touch one – it seemed only a bit smaller than his fingertip.

"What are these for?"

"Let me see," said Buharum, sidling past the others in the narrow hall and leaning in to take a closer look at some of the holes lower along the wall, at his own height. There were so many, they weren't hard to find. Dwarves always did pride themselves on topics like design and architecture, and clearly Buharum was no different.

But the Besak frowned and furrowed his bushy eyebrows. He huffed hard enough to kick up some dust from the walls.

"Damned if I know," said Buharum.

"Even I wouldn't be so flippant about self-damnation right now," said Djedar.

Buharum shrugged, then shivered. Dunewalker snorted.

"Maybe they shoot darts," Kukrum speculated. "They say the gods put traps in this place, and we know the tombs of some pharaohs are trapped for grave robbers. Why should a cursed and buried tomb be any different?"

"Awfully small for darts, brother," said Buharum, "and there are an awful *lot* of them. If it was darts, we'd be dead ten times over."

Kukrum just shrugged.

Djedar wasn't sure he believed it, either. Whatever their purpose, he saw them everywhere he looked, all very intentional and perfectly even.

They seemed to walk forever. Time dragged onward, as if reality itself had become warped. Perhaps it was from stress or fear, perhaps from the desperation of their mission, perhaps from every wall looking almost the same as the next... or perhaps it was part of the tomb's curse. A tomb so unimaginably vast could have itself been some trick of the gods, something else to torment Ankhu, making his labyrinth feel endless.

More and more, they ran across dead ends, trick pathways, and strange doors they could not open, sometimes splitting up only to find each other again soon afterward – or promptly backtrack and have to recover ground. Djedar almost began to feel sorry for Ankhu. No matter how evil or inhuman, such a place would drive anything insane or even madder than it already was.

Then, finally, they came to the most obvious fork in the path yet. Three passages stood before them, spread like the fingers of a trident: left, right, and center, none with any distinguishing markings. Dunewalker stopped and set his jaw again.

"I will take the center path," he said. "We need to split up again."

"Curse it, I don't like splitting up," Kukrum blurted. "We need to stick together if we're gonna stand a chance against that mummy whenever we find him."

"We need to cover more ground, Kukrum. We do not know how soon now the new moon will rise."

"Don't be afraid, brother," said Buharum, fishing into the pack on his back. "I'll take whatever path you do. Here, let's have a bit more light."

He brought out a stick of wood and quickly put together a rudimentary torch, which Dunewalker lit for him. Then the two dwarves took the right path, while Dunewalker walked down the center lane. Djedar alone went down the left passage, having to duck as the ceiling grew even closer and the walls closed in. He told himself this was only to rile fear in Ankhu during his monthly wanderings of his vast tomb...

Trouble was, it worked on him, too. Djedar felt tension creeping into him worse than ever as the walls came closer still, trying to box him in. Soon he found himself not only hunching but almost kneeling – then he had to return his sword to his belt, moving forward on his hands and knees. The torch's light revealed the passage only grew narrower ahead.

This was a trap.

Djedar froze. Cold sweat coated every inch of his skin, with more chilling him at the sight of how maddeningly, subtly narrower everything became.

Looking behind him felt like looking up the dark throat of some great monster as he willingly traveled deeper down its gullet like a brazen fool.

Then, ahead, he saw a strange light. Logic told him it was just another part of the trap, to make him crawl deeper and get stuck in the narrow passage, to be trapped and starve to death alone. But did the gods not respect those who didn't give in to fear – and reward them for their bravery?

Or was he only going to be punished for his stupidity?

Djedar took a breath and pressed onward, going down on his belly to crawl forward like a serpent, though he struggled to fit while dragging himself forward on his elbows – there simply wasn't enough space. His spine hurt. Pain shot up his arms whenever he tried to lift them straight out above his head.

He stopped. His body locked up; his arms no longer wanted to move. He'd pushed it too far. Djedar moaned and managed to drag his heavy arms back down to his sides. Whatever that monster in the Wastes had done to his back, this wasn't doing it any favors. He gripped the bottom of the torch between his teeth, knowing how stupid he looked carrying a torch lengthwise between his jaws, its flaming head poking more than a foot out from his face.

He tried using his feet instead, keeping his arms tucked in against his chest as he kept squeezing forward. He shoved himself along by his toes and heels, digging them into the stones behind him and pushing off. It was slow going, painstakingly so, letting him move only a few inches at a time. If the walls became any closer now, his shoulders would surely become wedged, and he'd have quite a time getting himself out—

Then, it opened up again.

The walls stopped narrowing. Djedar barely managed to fit through the remainder of the tunnel, shoving forward until his head found freedom and he dropped his torch into the next room. Stone scraped his bare skin, making him grimace as he shoved and wormed his shoulders through, practically spilling out from a perfectly rectangular hole in the wall and falling head-first into another open chamber.

Standing, he dusted himself off as best he could, snatching up his torch and looking around. Things looked the same as before, with depictions of the gods and strange scenes of Ankhu's lifetime covering the walls. For a place so dark, colors almost leapt out of the countless pictures surrounding him, and his torchlight shimmered off more gold along portions of the walls and ceiling.

Something glinted up ahead: the same shine he'd seen before. It looked almost like a glow rather than the gleam of a jewel catching the torchlight. No, this was another source of light but far too pale to be a simple flame. Whatever it was, it wasn't one of his companions.

Djedar kept walking. Though the passage cut off to his right, he saw a doorway straight ahead – but knew from experience the chamber was false. He had seen far too many during his time at the dig site.

Within shone the light he had seen before, however. Djedar couldn't resist taking a look.

A pale blue-white light filled the inside of the room. Leaning into the open chamber, he saw a crystal of some kind fitted into the ceiling. He squinted against the light it emitted, trying to better make it out. Perhaps it wasn't a crystal, though it had been cut so perfectly and polished to almost a mirror sheen that one could've been forgiven for the mistake.

It looked like... moonstone. He had seen moonstones before on jewelry, but never had he seen one glow.

Its illumination highlighted strange scarring across the floor, creating twisted shadows along the ground. Mismatched marks had been etched into the surface of the stone seemingly at random, lacking any of the beautiful symmetry of all the halls and chambers and perfectly-cut pillars throughout the tomb.

Acid. Djedar took a step back. Only acid could leave such designs in rock. He had seen it before, when some slaves had died to a trap that sprayed the burning chemical across their entire bodies and left them sizzling and screaming. He didn't plan to share their fate.

Who knew when exactly Ankhu had wandered into this chamber, only to be burned by acid, his undead form probably feeling the pain despite it causing no permanent damage. Djedar shuddered. Invincible, immortal... yet still suffering such agonies.

Not wanting to enter an obvious false chamber, Djedar made to leave and continue down the corridor to his right – but he paused. Something on the wall nearby caught his eye, something not quite like all the other symbols he had seen.

It was a sequence different from all the rest, underneath a unique image of a full moon over Anubis's uniquely-designed wolf head, his hands spread before him as he gazed down upon the earth. Words and phrases written in hieroglyphs surrounded him. Djedar recognized the sounds, though he wasn't sure what exactly they meant. They weren't like any words of Kemheti he had ever read or spoken, even after a lifetime spent speaking the language.

He murmured the syllables aloud under his breath – and the glow in the chamber beside him swelled.

Djedar's still-aching spine went stiff upon realizing the light was brighter than before. He stared at it, then back at the words – and tried to memorize them. These were no simple words. They were an incantation. They were *magic*. And if moonlight was what kept Ankhu at bay...

He spent a moment longer dedicating the incantation to memory. It had been written over and over across the walls like a warning in itself – or perhaps as a weapon, or even a taunt to Ankhu. Djedar understood nothing in this tomb nor why it had been arranged in such ways, but he deeply wished he could pry the stone from its place in the ceiling and keep it for himself, especially with his torch steadily beginning to falter.

Something moved.

After so long listening to nothing but that maddening heartbeat, at last hearing something else break the rhythm made Djedar start. Voices drifted down the passage – he recognized them. Dunewalker and Buharum must have met up again somewhere deeper within the tomb. Perhaps their paths had all met once again.

Djedar picked up the pace to reach them.

Buharum spun to face the footsteps that approached, brandishing his axe at – Djedar Rath. The former slave arrived from his own corridor, still carrying his torch, his body covered in sweat and dust and more than a few scrapes.

Djedar showed his free hand, taking a step back. "Easy," he said. "It's just me. Looks like our paths met up."

"So they did," replied Dunewalker, whom Buharum had found waiting for him here moments ago.

The entirety of the corridors Buharum and Kukrum had traveled led nowhere and revealed nothing but a few empty chambers – and always, *always* the infernal, incessant beating of Ankhu's damned heart. What could make one long for death more than to hate the sound of their own heartbeat? If that had been the gods' plans for Ankhu, Buharum thought they had succeeded.

"Glad you made it, Rath," Dunewalker added. "Looks like you ran into some trouble."

Djedar nodded. "I had an... encounter with a narrow passage. And I found something else, some kind of stone that emitted light. Pale light like the moon. Do any of you know something about that?"

Buharum shook his head, and Kukrum shrugged. It was Dunewalker who spoke after a moment of hesitation.

"Some tales claim moonlight can form into stones," he said. "But most aren't said to glow."

"Well, this one did."

"Maybe that means the moon's still up," said Kukrum. "Or the sun, or – something. Hopefully it means it's not the *new* moon yet, anyway."

Buharum scoffed. "For all I know the new moon's come and gone and Ankhu's already asleep again, as long as these halls feel. Who's to say he'd actually *find* the open door after waking up, anyway? Maybe all of this was stupid..."

They pressed on. The path ahead split yet again, but Dunewalker glanced over some hieroglyphs on the walls and then veered to the right. Everyone followed him wordlessly. Buharum offered silent thanks to his patron god Bes, hoping their little group wouldn't split up again.

Soon they passed beneath yet another entranceway. Statues of Anubis with eyes made of priceless rubies stood watchful on either side of this one – not an uncommon sight around here, save for those decorative eyes, but also not something which graced every single door. Buharum braced himself for the unexpected, but they walked right into the chamber beyond without any traps going off.

That chamber, however, was filled with the dead.

Dunewalker, Djedar, and Buharum all lifted their torches higher, scanning the walls lined with sarcophagi. The standing coffins had sculpted upon each lid an image of the person who rested within: all had their arms crossed over their chests – but the faces looked twisted, some with their mouths open, screaming in pain. Their hands were depicted as uneven, contorted and grasping at their own chests, their feet not at rest but folded over one another as if writhing in agony. Buharum could only imagine what the mummies within looked like, if the contents of those sarcophagi had even been given the grace of being mummified.

"Gods above," Buharum said quietly.

"Why give them the honor of mummification if it becomes a torture?" Djedar asked, his own voice low.

Dunewalker gave them a grim response: "These were Ankhu's most loyal men and priests of his order, buried with him in disgrace. Much like Tefnahkt has his slaves perceive him as a god, Ankhu's followers did the same. They revered him even over the Old Kingdom... they might have suffered a fate similar to Ankhu's own."

"Cursed as undead?" said Buharum. "But their sarcophagi wouldn't be shut."

"They might be too weak to escape. That doesn't mean they aren't still suffering."

Deeper in the room were several open tables, upon which rested two things each: an ancient clay goblet and a body wrapped in strips of linen. More mummies, but these weren't contained. Buharum stopped in his tracks.

"Well *those* are free," he remarked, feeling the color drain from his face.

But they didn't move. The longer he watched them, the more he suspected one of them was twitching, but he knew he was wrong. They were just that: mummies. Corpses. Bodies. They weren't going anywhere. Tales of the walking dead filled his imagination, as they had for all his long life, but he had never actually witnessed such a thing.

Buharum mentally admonished himself for being so fancifully paranoid and resumed searching the chamber with the others. Colorful images of horror stared back at him from everywhere he turned, but he saw no doors...

Something fell.

A clatter and a crash broke the stillness, making everyone start out of their skins. They whirled to face one of the tables, where a mummy still remained at rest – but the clay goblet had fallen from the edge, shattering on the floor.

No one moved.

"This is a dead end," Dunewalker said suddenly. "There are no exits here."

Then Buharum realized they were only three. Kukrum was gone.

"Where's Kukrum?" he blurted. "Where's my clan-brother?"

"He probably already left," said Djedar, not nearly concerned enough for Buharum's tastes, "like we should be doing."

The two Men made for the door, with Djedar in the lead, because Dunewalker strode Buharum's way to usher him out. But Buharum stood his ground, turning in another circle again. Maybe they'd just missed Kukrum; maybe he was behind one of those tall mummy tables—

"Kukrum!" Buharum called into the silent shadows. "Brother, where'd you go!?"

No response. Kukrum was gone.

"Buharum, we *must* leave—" Dunewalker urged, but Buharum wheeled on him and waved his torch almost in his face.

"Not until we find Kukrum! What if one of these things came alive and grabbed him and hauled him off!?"

Somewhere in the distant halls outside the mummy chamber, something clicked. Then— *slam.*

A deafening thud resounded over the thick stone walls, hard enough to shake dust from the ceiling. On the far side of the room, in the direction of their one way out, Djedar swore something vile in the Parsanshari language.

"We're trapped!" he called, whirling to face the inside of the chamber again and drawing the sword from his hip. What had once been the exit was now blocked by a sturdy face of decorated stone that barely looked out of place, as if the very walls of the tomb had shifted to seamlessly seal off this chamber and leave anyone outside clueless that it wasn't just a false doorway.

Silence fell once again, save for Ankhu's heart. Buharum wanted to let loose a wild cry and throw himself against the stone wall in search of escape, but he held it together. Still he looked everywhere for Kukrum, none of them daring to break the stillness again as they searched for a way out. Buharum kept throwing looks toward those mummies on the tables – but they never moved.

"Wherever you are, I hope you can get us out of here, brother," Buharum muttered under his breath as he went to a far wall and looked closely at its every stone, searching for any indication of a hidden lever or some crack out of place – somewhere Kukrum might've gone and some way they could escape, themselves...

Then a strange voice spoke. Deep and otherworldly, Buharum couldn't pinpoint its source. It echoed throughout the chamber, incanting strange words Buharum didn't understand. The very sound of those words being spoken seemed to suck from the room what little torchlight they had, as if each phrase brought with it so much evil that it threatened to banish all light from the world.

Dunewalker's ebony skin almost turned ashen, his lip twitching as if in disgust as his eyes roved the chamber for the source of the voice. He said under his breath, "The tongue of demons..."

It happened. What Buharum had feared all along came true.

One of the mummies snapped an arm straight up from its chest, reaching toward the so very distant heavens. It somehow pried its partially-wrapped jaw open enough to let loose a wretched, unnatural wail that would have stopped the heart of even the bravest warrior.

Another moved after it, this one faster. It sat up and leapt from the table, fingers splayed, ready to attack. A single uncovered pale eye stared out from the wrappings covering its dead face. Still more mummies climbed from their tables or practically fell sideways off them into unsightly heaps of ancient, twitching limbs, which rapidly began rearranging themselves and returning to feet they hadn't stood upon in countless ages.

They charged. Uncoordinated and nightmarish, some so contorted they could hardly move, the mummies picked their targets. Djedar's black khopesh swooped through the air to send one mummy flailing to the floor, but another quickly rose to replace it.

Buharum felt overwhelmed. A mummy came at him, its head on sideways, and he swung his crescent axe for its ankles. His blade sheared through the ancient flesh and bone, leaving the mummy standing on a single leg before Buharum knocked that one out from under it, too. The monster crashed to the floor in a pile of dust—

But it started to rearrange. From dust and decay, it swept back together to form the creature again – and the abomination turned its one-eyed head toward him, staring with all the hatred of over a thousand years' slumber.

"Aah – Dunewalker!" Buharum shouted. "They don't die!"

"They're already dead!" Djedar retorted, clearly terrified yet holding it together better than Buharum imagined he would. "How do you kill them *again!*?"

Dunewalker threw an undead off his blade before he answered. "We cannot! We must escape – Buharum, find us a way out!"

All because the blasted humans were too tall and didn't know their stone, it was *his* job to find a way out. Buharum would have complained or dropped a remark if he hadn't been so afraid for his life. As it was, he could only turn tail from the undead monstrosities making their way toward him and hurry straight back to the wall he'd been investigating before.

Nothing. Nothing at all – there were no cracks in this wall. The gods themselves had built this place, hadn't they? The *gods* didn't leave structural weaknesses—

A spindly, dead hand grasped at his arm from behind, tried to tug him off his feet. For something so ancient and brittle, it had strength Buharum hadn't expected. He toppled right over onto the ground to join a legless mummy there, nearly dropping his precious torch in the process.

Buharum shrieked, pulling away so hard the mummy's arm went with him. The creature let loose a guttural bellow, and Buharum tugged the hand off and threw it back at the mummy's head. Sand swirled behind the creature, starting to reform its legs...

A blade crashed down on the creature's neck – a black blade.

"Go, I'll keep them back!" barked Djedar. Dunewalker rushed toward them from across the chamber, coming to join in Buharum's defense.

Their protection made him feel frightfully important, which made the pressure much worse as Buharum returned his full attention to the wall. He looked everywhere – up, down, along the floor...

Near where the walls met, his torch shone oddly on a jagged shadow. A crack split through the stones there. It wasn't much, but maybe he could work with it.

Buharum scrambled for it, wedging his torch between some stones and one of the sarcophagi. He fought to remain steady while he set his axe aside and produced his hammer and chisel, setting to work widening the crack...

Dunewalker yelled. A wail from a mummy at his back made him wince. Djedar growled. Blades sheared ancient flesh and bone. All the while, Buharum kept his gaze fixed firmly on his chisel, hammer banging. The crack grew wider, stone falling away. The light from his torch nearby spilled out into another open space. He saw beyond into some kind of corridor, but he couldn't fit through the opening—

A boom shook the room and made Buharum knock his chisel awkwardly to one side. Finally risking a glance behind him, he saw one of the sarcophagus covers had fallen forward onto the floor. Out stepped a mummy, fully-formed, clad in a pectoral and helmet and lifting a sword from the tomb he left behind. This one looked far more formidable than the others.

They *were* guardians – they were more traps for trespassers. But who had awoken them? Or had they done that themselves? Had the voice from before been one of the gods, and if it was, why would the gods try to stop their own Medjai servants?

Buharum tossed his chisel aside and braced himself, starting to hammer away directly at the damaged stonework. Dust flew in his face and his eyes and tried to recolor his massive beard, but he worked himself an opening.

Djedar went down. Buharum heard him hit the ground just before he yelled in anger. Blades clashed afterward – yet still Buharum did not turn.

More stone fell away, almost too easily. But Buharum took his chance. Grabbing his torch and axe, he got down on his knees and crawled through the opening he made, leaving behind the sounds of battle and the death rattle of walking corpses.

He emerged into yet another of those same chilling hallways from before, the ones which felt so endless. Dunewalker's voice came from the room behind him—

"Buharum, *hurry!*"

Buharum didn't even have time to sneeze from all the dust in his beard. He clambered back to his feet and looked one way then the other, trying to figure out any differences at all, any signs of where to go... and he saw the faintest trail of dust leading straight down the hall, as if someone had recently passed this way. Following it and hoping he went the right way, Buharum set off at a run.

Familiar symbols stared out at him from the walls. Maybe he was just losing his mind, but he felt almost as if he knew where he was. It took him another turn, but he found it – the same passage they had traveled before. He was sure of it. He recognized the fork in the path.

Soon he found himself standing on the far side of the solid stone 'door' that had closed on them and sealed them in the chamber. Buharum glanced it up and down, wondering what in the gods' names to *do*, until he noticed something out of place.

The eyes of the statues were different. One red eye had receded into the left statue's head so far Buharum couldn't make it out. It seemed such a Dwarven thing for him to notice in the face of so much immediate danger and death, a gemstone looking different or being missing. He almost wanted to chide himself over it.

"Bes slap me if this really is important..." he muttered as he climbed up the statue.

Clambering high enough to reach the face of Anubis's wolf head, he shoved a thick finger into the eyehole until he found something and pressed down on it. A mechanism clicked. Slowly, the ruby eye started moving forward, back into position. With it, the wall that was actually a door slid away. Buharum clung to the long snout of the statue, lifting himself higher to look between the very tall, pointed ears atop the deity's head.

"Dunewalker! Rath!" he shouted. "The door!"

His words were unneeded. Dunewalker came stumbling out first, a streak of blood painting his chest, and Djedar quickly followed behind him. The instant they cleared the doorway, Buharum depressed the gem again, sending the stone sliding back into place—

And the wall slid with it. Staggering in Djedar's wake came one of the undead, but it would never make it – and then one of its more intact, faster counterparts tried to shove past, sword in hand, ancient teeth bared.

Djedar whirled in time to face it, landing a sudden, sharp kick right in the center of the mummy's chest. It flew back with a wail, falling hard in the doorway just in time for the stone door to smash it into dust.

The cry of the undead made Buharum shiver as the door thudded back into place with heavy finality, crushing the ancient mummies caught in its path and perhaps finally destroying some for good. Or maybe they could reassemble themselves the instant the door was opened – Buharum didn't want to find out.

At long last, silence fell once again... except for the endless heartbeat, eternal and unchanging, wanting to make Buharum's ears explode with its persistence.

"Hope they can't fit through that hole in the wall," Buharum muttered as he climbed down off the statue of Anubis. Djedar and Dunewalker had more than a few slashes on them, and it looked like someone had clubbed Dunewalker in the head, but they didn't seem too worse for wear.

"Thank you," Dunewalker said. "We were being overwhelmed."

Buharum gave a wave. "Don't mention it. But Kukrum wasn't in there or anywhere in the halls nearby. We gotta find him."

Dunewalker was tired of the dark.

He led the way as they strode ever deeper into the endless, time-stretching halls of Ankhu's tomb, back on the move again after their encounter with the mummies. The gashes over his chest and marring his left arm stung and burned in the warm, stuffy air that felt closer than ever.

Suffocation somehow felt like a very real possibility, as far underground as they were – especially with Ankhu's heart pounding in his ears along with his own, doubling the sound, making him feel as though he could barely catch his own breath. He tried not to think about it.

Holding his torch aloft for so long had left even his strong arms aching for relief, and now that one of them bled, he only felt worse. Yet still he pressed on, scarcely wasting time to look behind him and make sure the sets of quiet footsteps in his wake were his two companions instead of undead abominations seeking to kill him.

No one spoke. No one needed to. Everything had left them so weary that all energy had to be poured into their singular purpose: stopping Tefnahkt. Dunewalker wondered now if they would even be able to escape and re-seal the tomb before Ankhu awakened or if this venture would cost them their lives.

A light flashed ahead, faint in the distant corridor. Bright red-orange it was, like a powerful flame. Dunewalker halted, staring.

"Kukrum!" Buharum called, stepping forward, but Dunewalker reached down to put a hand on his shoulder.

"Use caution, old friend," he warned. "We don't know it's him."

"It's *got* to be – he's still down here somewhere!"

Dunewalker didn't answer. Judging by the dark look he received from Djedar, they were thinking the same thing: Kukrum had probably run afoul of a trap somewhere.

The light went out, as quickly as it had appeared.

"*Brother!*" Buharum shouted – and he ran.

"Buharum, wait!"

It was no use. Buharum took off faster than Dunewalker had ever given his short legs credit for. Dunewalker didn't hesitate to follow, Djedar hot on his heels. They cleared the length of the corridor and came upon yet another doorway, this one with bright red-orange lights cresting beyond it in what looked like a sequence.

Then, even Buharum stopped. The lights ahead had gone dark. Dunewalker found himself on a set of stairs leading a short way down into a long, open room – more open than any room they had encountered so far.

On every single wall, everywhere he looked, he saw nothing but words of warning. Talk of Ankhu's endless evil, of curses, of the swallowing sands of the desert and the fires of the Underworld itself.

There, on the floor before them, lay Kukrum's hammer and chisel, identical to Buharum's own. Dunewalker frowned as Buharum stepped toward them, kneeling to pick them up and turn them over in his hands.

"Buharum..." Dunewalker started.

"I *know*," Buharum snapped. "I'm not a child, Dunewalker. I've been around longer than the two of you put together, remember?"

Sometimes I wonder, Dunewalker thought, but he didn't voice it.

"Try losing *your* clan-brother in this wretched place," Buharum muttered. "Though Kemhetis don't have such clans..."

He started walking forward. Dunewalker followed him, and Djedar came last. As they neared the bottom of the stairs, shapes spread out before them on the floor – symbols Dunewalker immediately recognized.

The names of gods and of virtues and sins had been carved into various tiles, one word for each, composed of their hieroglyphs. The falcon of Horus caught Dunewalker's eye first. Scattered among those gods and deeds of good and evil, out of place amidst so many deities, was the name of Ankhu.

Each stone looked uneven. Such imperfection stood out against the smooth and symmetrical stonework surrounding them.

"I don't like this," said Buharum.

Djedar appeared by Dunewalker's side, carefully reaching out with one foot. Leaning his body away from the stone, he stretched his leg out to press down on it with as much distance as he could. The stone gently sank until it was level with the floor...

And a massive gout of flame like the breath of a dragon burst forth from a statue's maw to their left, spraying an inferno across a portion of the room, only narrowly missing Djedar. He stumbled back, grimacing.

"So that was the light we saw," Buharum said. "But the room looks empty. Do you think Kukrum passed this way?"

"Could have been Tefnahkt," speculated Djedar. "We saw the fires, like someone walked through the room – there must be a way through on the other side."

Dunewalker nodded. "This is almost certainly the way forward. But this is no ordinary flame. The walls talk of the Underworld's own fires. If this fire touches you, I am not sure we could put it out."

"Dammit," Buharum swore, swinging his torch in an arc. *Kukrum!* he called again, to no response. Then he drew himself up as much as a dwarf his size could, his massive beard puffing out with his barrel chest. He strode toward the stones, looking over them.

"This is the tale of Ankhu," Dunewalker said. "But the first row of stones are only the names of the gods... and Ankhu was unholy."

"Horus guarded many chambers we found in the dig site," Djedar pointed out. "He overlooked the treasure chamber."

Dunewalker frowned. Horus was the god of vengeance, and it was true he'd appeared throughout the tomb... but he was also Djedar's favored deity, from what Dunewalker could gather. Some bias had to be taken into account.

He asked, "What gods have we seen who subdued Ankhu?"

"That's not the *start* of the story," Buharum cut in. "If this is the start, I'm going with the god I've seen everywhere I turn in this blasted place. Seen enough statues of him now to carve one from memory."

And, before anyone could stop him or even speak, Buharum stepped on the tile depicting a set of hieroglyphs: a feather, a bird, a wolf on a pedestal, among others... the name of Anubis, judge of the dead.

The tile stayed in place. Buharum deflated on the spot, seeming a good two inches narrower by the time he finished exhaling in relief.

But Dunewalker scowled – he didn't understand. That made no sense. "This didn't begin with Anubis...

did it? How could it— it began with *demons*. Ankhu was a spawn of a devil."

"Perhaps," said Djedar, "Anubis was the first to try to stop it."

Dunewalker hoped that was true. He went next, following after Buharum and taking a place on the Anubis tile, while Buharum himself moved on seamlessly to a tile bearing Ankhu's name.

Slowly, tile by tile, they made their way across the room. No more jets of flame interrupted their passage. The Medjai knew much of Ankhu's history: his name, how he began as a vizier in Waset, the many titles he took up after the start of his conquest...

It all made sense, as difficult as some tiles were to reach. The only one out of place so far was to start with Anubis. The gods had nothing to do with Ankhu's rise to power. They were the ones who *stopped* him.

Suddenly, Buharum's progress came to a halt. He looked back at them, confusion written over his thickly bearded face, and he said, "These are sins. Malice, fury, pride... what comes next?"

"What powers did Ankhu possess?" Djedar asked. "Or does anyone know that?"

"We know of a few," Dunewalker replied. "He could create sandstorms, raise the dead..."

From the darkness behind them, another voice answered.

"Famine. He could create plagues of devouring insects."

Kukrum.

"Brother!" Buharum called out into the dark, almost taking another step forward off the safety of his tile. "Are you alright? Where are you?"

"I'm quite fine, brother," said Kukrum, still swathed in distant shadow so Dunewalker couldn't make him out. "It's you who aren't."

A weight fell into the pit of his stomach. Dunewalker set his jaw. Buharum's face grew blank as though his entire world crushed inward.

He asked almost meekly, "What are you talking about, clan-brother?"

"We all have that person... that person we confide in above all others." Kukrum's voice began to drift as he walked toward the left side of the room at their backs, behind them, safe from the trapped tiles. Dunewalker followed his voice despite being unable to see him, and he threw a look back at the grim-faced Djedar, who only nodded to indicate he was prepared for anything.

"The person we trust," Kukrum continued, "to hear our grievances. Even complaints about our own family – siblings, parents... lovers. Best friends. The secrets we keep. And always we confide in someone above all others. The nicest, most trustworthy. With them, we can share *anything*. Can't we?

"But how do you know they aren't listening to your every complaint, your every *whine*, your every dark secret, and collecting all this dishonesty and malcontent and *dirt*, laughing about it behind your back? Using it against you, knowing precisely how to drive wedges amidst a group, how best to trap you when the time is right? To throw you away when you've spent your use, then spin tales of how *you* were the heartless liar?"

"Brother..." Buharum started, despair driving his voice almost into a high and broken whine, but Kukrum still wasn't finished.

"*I* was that friend," he said. "I was that person for so many. Everyone trusted kind little Kukrum. 'The nice one.' It's so damn easy to be '*nice*.' All you have to do is speak some meaningless platitudes, words of unhelpful kindness, and waste too many hours with them. How long I languished in the Medjai, watching their self-righteousness. They think they serve the gods, as Solon believed he served Ra – where was *Ra* when Tefnahkt destroyed such a wonderful servant?"

"No!" Buharum suddenly bellowed, his voice echoing off every corner of the room. "This isn't *possible* – you're a Besak! A holy servant of Bes— none of us would ever turn away from what's right and honest!"

Kukrum laughed. The sound made even Dunewalker close his eyes, lowering his head in pain. This wasn't the voice of the dwarf he had trusted all his life. It *couldn't* be.

"I waited for so long, Buharum," Kukrum said. "The others thought I could never get the Medjai to trust me. But I waited and worked my way deeper into you supposed holy servants of the Old Kingdom— these weakling gods so terrified by their own power and curses that they sealed Ankhu away and tormented him just for using the tools he was *given*. And the gods of Parsanshar, equally as pathetic, locked in their blind war imagined between light and dark.

"Finally," he finished, "my time has come. And the only thing... the *only* thing that matters – is *time*."

With those words, everything fell into place. An ancient order, now fallen, chased to the corners of the world and hiding in the darkness, believing in neither good nor evil, neither order nor chaos, believing only in power and the endless march of the ages...

The Zharduvari. Time was all they thought about – the decay of time and the solution to defeating it: immortality.

Kukrum was like Tefnahkt. He was a Zhar.

"Ammit will still destroy your soul," Djedar snarled.

"No, slave," Kukrum said through a sneer Dunewalker could hear but not witness, "your gods will never find me. But they will soon find *you*."

A crossbow loosed in the darkness. The bolt came so suddenly they had no time to prepare – and nowhere to go to avoid it.

It struck Buharum in the shoulder, knocking him off-balance. Dunewalker lunged to catch him before he could fall into another plate in the floor – but a second bolt quickly followed the first. It grazed Dunewalker's leg with a sear of hot pain, and he lost his footing.

He plunged right onto an incorrect stone, one large enough that his entire body didn't cover the extent of its surface. He landed on it with his full weight. It immediately began sinking into the floor. But no gout of flame shot forth to burn him alive, and the stone sank deeper— and deeper, until Dunewalker realized he was rapidly disappearing into a hole.

Sand. It spilled inward around him, coming from nowhere, filling the area around him and over the stones just around his head. And like everything else in this place of magic and curses, it was no ordinary sand.

It clung to him, weighed him, pulling on Dunewalker's limbs and trying to drag him down with the already-disappeared stone he'd landed upon. He reached up, grabbing for the edges of the opening – but his fingers slipped. And still the stone beneath his feet plummeted ever lower, the sand rising above his waist.

Sounds of battle rang out over his head, but Dunewalker couldn't see. He scrabbled at the edge of the hole, trying to find purchase, trying at least to get his fingers on the edge and pull himself up...

But he couldn't.

Then a hand appeared, too large to be Buharum's and without his thick stumpy fingers, belonging to an arm far longer than a dwarf's. Djedar knelt over the edge of the opening, reaching down.

"Take my hand!" Djedar called, and Dunewalker struggled to reach in the clinging sand.

It wasn't enough – his fingers barely brushed Djedar's fingertips, and still the sand engulfed him. He could feel himself being swallowed by it, his feet no longer touching stone but sucking into thick murkiness.

Djedar dropped flat onto his chest, stretching as far as he could, his hand finally snatching Dunewalker's. Sand began to fill Dunewalker's mouth, his nose, his eyes— he couldn't see, couldn't breathe, couldn't hear, he could only *feel* – feel himself going ever deeper, farther from the light and the air. Drowning.

Then he felt a pull.

Djedar tugged with all his might, his injured spine wanting to crush inward on itself. He planted his feet and bared his teeth, holding tight onto the glimpse of Dunewalker's dark hand that still desperately clung to him. The sand pulled back, not wanting to give up its prey—

But Dunewalker's head finally came up. He sputtered and gasped. His other arm appeared next, lurching free of the sand and shooting up to grab hold of Djedar's wrist as they both kept pulling.

And, barely a few feet away in the chamber, Buharum's axe sang wildly through the air.

"How *dare* you, you *swine!*" Buharum bellowed. "You betrayed all we stand for – we fought and bled together! We watched our friends and our clan-brothers die! And all this time, all these decades, you felt *nothing!?*"

Djedar didn't hear any payoff. Buharum's axe met neither armor nor flesh. Kukrum must have escaped.

Yet they still heard the traitor dwarf's voice: "I'm only surprised you didn't see that mechanism when we first came upon the chamber with the dead priests, brother. But then you always were better with your silly little chisel than you were with engineering— were you impressed when I woke the undead?"

"*Warlock*," Buharum hissed.

Dunewalker was almost free now. His shoulders came loose, and Djedar rearranged his footing, bracing harder.

Then something wailed. A blade struck Djedar across in the arm, leaving lancing pain and hot blood in its wake. He staggered forward, costing Dunewalker several inches of freedom. Looking over his shoulder, a mummy stared back at him – one of the same walking dead from the chamber they'd escaped before. So at least some of them *had* found the hole Buharum had used to escape.

But Dunewalker grabbed hold of Djedar's shoulders and, with a massive heave, hauled himself out of the sand. He slammed headlong into the mummy, driving it back onto one of the safe tiles, wrestling the creature for its sword.

Another mummy charged forward, so lightweight – composed of little more than ancient bone and flesh and wrappings – that it didn't even trigger the depression of the trapped tiles. Djedar wheeled to face it, drawing his black blade just in time to catch the undead's sword on his own.

Blade ground against blade, but Djedar twisted and pulled them free, bringing his khopesh back around to hack at the mummy's side. The creature staggered yet barely seemed to feel it, swinging its own sword – but again Djedar deflected, taking a step back. And onto a different stone.

The floor beneath his feet began to sink... but not far.

Djedar dropped. He fell onto his side, but he lifted his torch up to what he thought would be only just enough—

Fire bellowed forth from the open, toothy maw of a towering statue of the lion-headed goddess Sekhmet, standing guard over the tiled floor. Flames engulfed the mummy in an instant, wrapping it in an inferno. Djedar remained where he was, watching as the creature wailed and flailed, filling the air with the stink of burning ancient flesh and bandages. It staggered only briefly before rapidly beginning to dissipate, until all that remained was a pile of dust.

It didn't recompose itself. It was gone. And his torch burned with a flame brighter than he had ever seen.

"Dunewalker!" Djedar shouted, scrambling off the tile and then leaping to his feet. "The fire's holy – it will destroy them!"

A cry rang out. Djedar looked up to see Buharum staggered on one leg, put on the defensive. He wrestled with Kukrum, their axes identical, each trying to gain an upper hand.

"Go!" Dunewalker ordered, standing his ground against another undead. "Help him – I can handle these!"

"Use this!" Djedar tossed him his torch, glowing bright with holy flame. The moment Dunewalker caught it, Djedar took off across the tiles.

He leapt over one then the other, his footing quick and sure. Two more mummies, much slower than the first, made their way toward him. The creatures stalked across the floor, heedless of the gods' traps and warnings. Djedar delivered a swift round kick to one's skull, knocking its head off and removing it from his path. He avoided the other creature altogether, sights set on the battle between the two dwarven clan-brothers.

Kukrum won their struggle. Pulling his weapon free, he brought the butt around to slam into Buharum's face – then whirled and hefted the blade instead, slashing across his head. Buharum went down with a yell, dropping his axe, hands over his face and his helmet now askew. Djedar couldn't be sure Buharum hadn't just been blinded – or worse.

Kukrum would die either way.

Djedar rushed him, blade in hand, teeth bared. Kukrum wheeled on him instantly, axe up to catch his strike. A wicked grin shone against the blackness of Kukrum's great beard, his dark eyes glittering in the light of Buharum's since abandoned torch that rested on the floor nearby.

Djedar pulled his sword free and struck again – and again. Kukrum was a skilled warrior. Every move Djedar made, he saw coming and deflected it. The dwarf swung his own heavy blows with his crescent axe, but Djedar leapt back or pushed them away with his sword.

"You're a better fighter than your birth had me believe!" Kukrum remarked. "Who taught you, slave? Was it Tefnahkt?"

"*Har-em-akhet* gave me skill so I could kill you when this time came," Djedar snarled back.

Kukrum scoffed, knocking Djedar's khopesh away yet again. "Cry Horus's name and ask him for help, then – or are you afraid he won't answer?"

Blade against blade sounded again. Steel and void iron rang out, deafening, blending with the steady beat of Ankhu's cursed heart – and Djedar's own heart, which raced in his ears. And he did what Kukrum had dared him to do, reciting a mental prayer for Horus to make him his weapon and allow him to carry out vengeance upon this traitor.

Kukrum broke through. Djedar's defense faltered – and Kukrum saw his chance. He knocked Djedar's sword aside with enough force to make an opening, rushing forward and slamming into Djedar's nearest leg like a battering ram.

Despite being knocked off-balance, Djedar didn't fall, stumbling back a few paces – and then he felt the earth sinking beneath him. Kukrum had forced him back onto the trapped tiles. Deeper the stone went, falling rapidly away and taking him with it. Sand, thick and viscous and strange, spilled in around his feet.

Djedar didn't hesitate. He had nowhere to go, so he climbed right out – and right into Kukrum's waiting blade.

Only no blade came for him.

Someone rushed Kukrum from the side, stopping him from attacking the vulnerable Djedar. Buharum, his face covered in blood, struck Kukrum in the shoulder. The blow didn't pierce his thick armor, but it did distract him and give Djedar time to escape the pit.

Kukrum spat a curse, but Buharum did not relent. He struck again and again, driving Kukrum back pace by pace...

Until he stumbled back into the sand, so thick he couldn't lift his boots free. It spilled into the hole left by the sinking stone, dragging Kukrum along with it. Kukrum yelled in rage, struggling, but it was no use. He couldn't pull his stocky limbs free as the sand swept him back toward the hole and rapidly dragged him downward.

Again he yelled, roaring like a madman. He hefted his axe and threw it. It sailed straight for Buharum, but the other dwarf knocked it out of the air with his matching weapon. Face cold as ice, Buharum stepped closer to the pit of cursed quicksand, staring at his former clan-brother.

Djedar straightened up and scanned the chamber – the mummies were gone. The room was as still as before, filled with Ankhu's heartbeat. No fires flashed, no mummies wailed. There was only him, Buharum, Dunewalker making his way back toward them with his holy torch... and Kukrum sinking ever faster into the swallowing sand.

Kukrum gnashed his teeth, still trying to pull free, now submerged just beyond his arms. "You'll all die," he snarled. "You're no match for Tefnahkt. Do you even know what he's sacrificed for so much power? He'll awaken Ankhu and take *his* power, too. If you go now, maybe you'll reach him just in time to watch."

No one spoke. Djedar looked at Buharum for an answer. But he only stood, watching as the sand swallowed up his clan-brother who had betrayed them all.

Finally, Buharum said slowly, "You were my family, Kukrum. Do you even know what that means?"

"No. I *have* no brothers," Kukrum snapped. "I *have* no family. Family means nothing – family can't save you from what's coming."

Buharum set his axe aside and took the crossbow from his back, loading a bolt. "I did have a brother in you, Kukrum, even if you never felt the same. Consider this my last act of brotherhood: showing you mercy you don't deserve."

Just as the sand threatened to envelop Kukrum's skull, to drown him slowly and painfully, Buharum leveled his crossbow for Kukrum's head...

Djedar turned away. He heard the crossbow go off, but he didn't watch. Instead, he took up Buharum's torch and made his way across the tiles he knew were safe. Now was no time for drawn-out sorrows.

They continued in silence across the trapped floor. The final tile, as it turned out, read 'Anubis' yet again. Dunewalker looked disturbed by this, and Djedar felt the same. He had at times looked to Anubis as well as Horus, seeking guidance and favor from him. If Anubis had something to do with everything that had happened here... what did it mean? Anubis was no *evil* deity, despite what some foreigners liked to assume – was he?

Only when they found themselves walking down still more tomb hallways did Buharum finally break.

"My own brother," he suddenly wailed, "a Zharduvar – a *cultist!* How? Why? How did none of us *see* this?"

"He took us all by surprise, Buharum," Dunewalker said almost cautiously, but Buharum hardly seemed to hear.

"The Besak are corrupted— the Zhar reached us somehow. If they can reach one of us, how many others have taken up their ways? We dedicated ourselves to everything holy – and Kukrum and I dedicated ourselves to the Medjai. Servants of the gods, a holy order – how could the *gods* allow this?"

Buharum's voice kept rising. He cried his laments louder still, until Dunewalker wheeled and knelt before the dwarf, putting his hands on Buharum's shoulders.

"I know it's hard, my friend," said Dunewalker, "but compose yourself. Kukrum is gone. The Besak you thought you knew never existed – he was a lie. There are many lies in this world. Sometimes even the people we care for most are nothing but lies, themselves."

Buharum actually sobbed. Just once, but it was ugly. His entire body gave a violent jerk, his eyes full of tears.

"He was my *brother*, Dune," Buharum moaned. "I trusted him with... with *everything*."

Dunewalker nodded. "I know, Buharum. I trusted him as well. But we cannot stay here and tend to our grief. The new moon will rise any minute now. Darkness will fill the sky, and the stars alone cannot keep Ankhu at rest."

It took a moment longer, but Buharum gathered his dignity. He lifted a portion of his enormous beard to wipe his eyes and some of the blood from his face, drawing in a stuttering breath. Then he cleared his throat and waved away Dunewalker, who rose reluctantly.

After that, they continued. Yet again they walked down seemingly endless halls only to suddenly see a light at the end, straight ahead. It glowed pale and blue-white like the moon, like the stone Djedar had seen in the chamber before.

The walls here looked almost blank, showing only depictions of the phases of the moon, always with the empty new moon in the center. Set in those walls around the moon phases were facets holding stones large enough to fit in the palm of a man's hand. They were pale, almost white, and glowed with an inner light of pure magic as bright as moonlight itself.

A square doorway stood in their only path forward, looking into a great room of darkness with only a single dim and distant light within. A single word had been written in hieroglyphs across the top of the entrance...

'ANKHU.'

Of all the warnings, of all the curses and many names and symbols and strange stories told across the boundless walls of the tomb, seeing the legendary pharaoh's name stand on its own chilled Djedar to the bone. He stared up at it for a moment as if unable to move.

This was it. Beyond this doorway lay the resting place of one of the single greatest evils that had ever walked the mortal realm.

"I suppose the tales of some moonstones and their light are true," Dunewalker remarked, gazing at one of the glowing stones in the wall. Djedar looked at one as well. "Some say they reflect the heavens, only glowing when the sun or moon is shining."

"They must carry that light down here and keep Ankhu asleep," Buharum pointed out in a mutter.

Djedar reached out and ran his fingers along the surface of the stone nearest him. It was smooth, pleasant to the touch, but cold. It emitted light but no heat.

"I may have found a way to use them," he said. "An incantation."

Buharum's eyebrows rode high on his face at the thought. Without a word, he reached into his pack and took out something, offering it up to him: Kukrum's a hammer and chisel. Djedar accepted them and setting to work freeing the stone from its facet. It fell into Buharum's waiting hands, and the dwarf passed that up to him, as well.

"If you think you *can* make this thing glow whenever you please, might as well use every edge we can get," Buharum said. "We're gonna need it."

Djedar only nodded. Then, still haunted as ever by the beating of the heart, they each turned back to the entrance awaiting them and strode beyond the threshold... into the resting place of Ankhu himself.

The light of a single torch burned ahead, barely able to penetrate the heavy shadows that blanketed the vast burial chamber of Pharaoh Ankhu himself. Dunewalker and Djedar still carried their own torches, Dunewalker's burning with holy flame. Only the light from his blessed torch truly dismissed the seemingly unnatural darkness that pervaded the area, save for the distantly lit regions of the room where holy moonlight touched the corners.

Where every other chamber had been covered with nigh-upon countless hieroglyphs and other imagery of gods and the history of Ankhu, the walls and ceiling of this chamber were utterly barren, as desolate as the Wastes. After all they had seen for so long, it looked stark and frightening. Not even words of a curse was written to Ankhu in this chillingly empty room, empty and alone – void of any communication, any symbols, any magic, any presence of the gods...

Moonstones glowing bright blue-white had been fixed into the far walls in this chamber as well. But they offered little direct light in the center, where a shroud of pure blackness reached forth from Ankhu's sarcophagus as if the thing within was so terrible, so powerful, so cursed that no light could touch it...

Which was exactly why Tefnahkt's torch did little to aid him in seeing what it was he'd so eagerly sought.

There he was: the warlock Lord Tefnahkt the Red, leaned over the sarcophagus and clad in his same long red robes as before, his back turned to them. His torch, about to go out, rested in a previously empty mount anchored to the floor near Ankhu's resting place.

Suddenly, Tefnahkt the Red stood upright and wheeled to face them. His weary face looked decades older than it had during the battle at his fortress. Pale skin glistened with sweat in the dim torchlight, glinting off the metal beard jutting from his chin. Tefnahkt's entire visage was sickly and shriveled, his cheeks sunken, unlike the proud man from before. To defeat Solon, he had drawn too much power at once from the demon he served – and it had taken fragments of his soul as payment. Such a sacrifice always left a mark.

He lifted a hand, veins dark and prominent, and held it aloft to summon his evil power in a moment's notice.

"And how," said Tefnahkt, "do you three whelps imagine you'll face me without your precious channeler? Two Medjai and a slave – preposterous."

Buharum balked, inching back, but Dunewalker took one strong stride forward and bared his broad chest. "You cannot control Ankhu's power, Tefnahkt," he declared. "I do not know what you're planning here tonight, but surely you must know Ankhu will never submit to you!"

"He need not 'submit.' I will *break* him."

"You believe yourself capable of breaking one the gods themselves descended to subdue?" said Djedar, stepping forward alongside Dunewalker. Finally, after that, Buharum reluctantly sidled forth to join them as well.

"I 'believe' nothing," said Tefnahkt. Dunewalker saw crimson-hued shadows bend and twist around the warlock's fingertips. "I *know*. Now face the same fate as your captain!"

Light flashed – or perhaps darkness flashed and the light bent and warped trying to overtake it. Red-black tendrils like otherworldly flame sprang from Tefnahkt's hand, but the Medjai scattered. His power was not so quick and relentless as before, weak as he was.

Dunewalker did not hesitate. He charged forward, weapon at the ready, and ascended the platform upon which Ankhu's sarcophagus rested, lunging for Tefnahkt and striking true—

But his blade glanced off something invisible, like a shield he couldn't see. Tefnahkt gnashed his teeth at him with an almost demonic hiss, even more light fading from his eyes as his magic shield was struck. He clearly used his own soul to form it, as well.

"Without your channeler, you are *nothing*," Tefnahkt hissed, lifting his hand once more.

Before Dunewalker had time to move, the magic struck him. Tendrils of crimson red mingled with twisted shadow that ate the light hit him full in the chest. Cold filled every inch of his body for a moment, so cold he thought he had surely died on the spot.

Dunewalker fell away, off the platform and flat on his back, gasping for breath. Pain came afterward, twisting into him, making him shake all over so hard he could barely grip his weapon or his torch... and then Tefnahkt stepped forward, standing over him, filling his vision. A stone came from nowhere, a rock thrown by someone – Buharum, perhaps – trying to get Tefnahkt away from

Dunewalker's paralyzed form. But the stone bounced off the invisible shield, and Tefnahkt ignored it entirely.

Tefnahkt lifted his hand to take Dunewalker's life with a simple wave, a flick, as if dismissing a flea...

Djedar leapt.

The solid black blade of his khopesh sang through the air – and found no shield at all. Only void iron could pierce magic or even absorb it, and now Blacksword's own weapon would be his master's undoing.

The sword struck Tefnahkt directly in the neck. He staggered off-balance with a wretched yell, his hand that had been poised to kill Dunewalker shooting up to clutch the wound instead. The warlock hissed again and wheeled to face his new foe: one of his own slaves.

"You," Tefnahkt said through a sneer, drawing a sword from his belt and falling into a battle stance. "You *scum*. I should have had you killed along with your family—"

"Yes," Djedar said simply, "you should have. Sparing me will become your greatest regret – if only briefly."

"What was it like to be so powerless?" Tefnahkt said, circling behind Ankhu's massive, blank sarcophagus of solid black. "Or could you even see your whelp's blood in that sandstorm?"

A vicious smile tugged at Djedar's lips. "How are you so confident that they died at all, 'master?' How many slave-drivers did you lose that day? Do you really think the storm alone took so many lives?"

Tefnahkt didn't answer, narrowing his eyes.

Still he tried to keep the sarcophagus between the two of them. Djedar struggled not to let him gain any ground while trying keep his distance from the coffin. It was difficult to focus through the unnatural shadow that threatened to swallow them both, close as they were to Ankhu's cursed body...

For the briefest moment, Tefnahkt stumbled. His strength failed him; he misstepped on the platform of the sarcophagus, and Djedar saw his chance.

Up he leapt, right onto Ankhu's resting place, his blade sailing for Tefnahkt's head. But though the warlock was weak, he reacted quickly, catching Djedar's blade on his own. He staggered backward, out of reach, and Djedar charged. He all but fell forward off the sarcophagus, his movement swift and graceful, blade still swinging.

Again Tefnahkt caught the blow, twisting his own weapon free, but Djedar did not relent. He struck again and again, his method not the most skilled or practiced – but full of such fury that Tefnahkt was forced on the defensive. He easily parried each swing of Djedar's sword with all the skill of a master swordsman. Djedar would never win like this.

Suddenly, Tefnahkt threw forward his free hand, once again summoning dark magic. Djedar brought his black blade to bear, but it was only a weapon. Djedar watched as the impossible red-black tendrils of demonic power flowed around the narrow void iron blade to reach him.

Agony erupted through his body. It spread like fire but without heat, blasting his every nerve. Weakness flowed through him like ice water. Fear filled his mind, blinding him, and his chest felt full of clay. He couldn't breathe, suffocating under nothing but twisting pain and sheer terror.

He collapsed as the cold rushed into him, reaching his very core. Barely able to lift his heavy eyelids, Djedar managed to look up at the warlock who stood over him. Tefnahkt took a step forward, hand extended, dark magic still flowing from him. He focused all his energy, the dim crimson glow of his power pulsing. Then Djedar realized it, realized what Tefnahkt was doing...

The pallor of Tefnahkt's skin began to brighten, as if given new life. The sheen over his eyes lifted like fog clearing after a storm. With all of it, Djedar felt ever weaker, slumping forward on his hands and knees as Tefnahkt stole his very life-force. Djedar could not fight it. He could not stop it. Men had no power against magic.

He had been a fool to come here, to ever imagine fighting a warlock, to think for a moment he could do good instead of running off into the desert like he should've from the start—

Suddenly, the moonstones went out.

Darkness enveloped them. Enveloped *everything*. Even the pain that had clouded Djedar's entire being disappeared at once as Tefnahkt started back in surprise. Still Djedar couldn't move, feeling cold and strange, his hands trembling. The unnatural fear that had clouded his every thought was only just now starting to truly fade.

The silence crushing inward around them took their breath away. Almost every ounce of light was gone. The ordinary torch went out, as if all things good and right in the world had been extinguished, for no light could survive against the powerful shadow that the moonstones alone had held back—

No light except the holy flame still burning in the torch that Dunewalker held. It was only from that singular light that they all witnessed a legend come true.

A crack like thunder split the air. Stone scraped against stone – and in the thick shadow, Djedar saw the lid of the coffin move.

From the shadows of the nearby sarcophagus, Djedar scarcely made out a creature rotten and hideous, towering unnaturally large, shreds of tattered wrappings hanging from its lanky and nearly skeletal form. He was too tall and his limbs too long, like some gangling nightmare. In the flickering flame, Djedar caught a glimpse of a skull with but a few scraps of ancient flesh still clinging to ancient, dusty bone. Yet still this abomination wore an elaborate headdress, the royal *nemes* of a true ruler of Kemhet.

Before them now stood the awakened undead form, the walking mummy, of Pharaoh Ankhu the Endless.

Tefnahkt rose at once, straightening himself with newfound strength stolen from Djedar. He ascended the stairs to Ankhu's sarcophagus with no fear of the terrible being that gazed upon him with empty pits for eyes.

"Pharaoh Ankhu!" Tefnahkt bellowed in command. "I have freed you from your prison – and now you shall serve *me!*"

Dark magic sprung forth from Tefnahkt's outstretched hands, rushing toward Ankhu and twisting the shadows around the great mummy into otherworldly hues of crimson. But Ankhu merely lifted one long, bony hand, and the magic dissipated before it ever reached him.

Tefnahkt paused, eyes wide – but he did not relent. With a wild yell, he summoned still more, quickly relinquishing what he stole from Djedar and sacrificing it for demonic power. Red shadows and light alike filled the chamber, centered around the warlock. Tefnahkt's eyes became pits of flame once more as he thrust his hands forward, sending all his unholy might toward the silhouetted form of Ankhu...

It didn't matter. Ankhu took one step forward, and all the demonic energy flowed away from him like water around a stone. With a flick of his hand, he dismissed every ounce of Tefnahkt's incredible power.

Tefnahkt had only long enough to scream in horror before Ankhu's skeletal hand wrapped around his throat. The mummy effortlessly lifted him from his feet, holding him aloft. In the shadows that swarmed around Ankhu's feet and still recovering from his weakened state, Djedar saw little... but he also saw enough.

Tefnahkt screamed and writhed in Ankhu's grasp. The undead pharaoh did not react, a deep rattle and a hiss escaping from between the ancient teeth of his skull—

And Tefnahkt seemed to light up from within, a blinding white glow that suddenly spilled forth from his mouth, his eyes, everything, so bright Djedar covered his face and looked away. Louder Tefnahkt screamed, only to suddenly be silenced.

When Djedar dared look again, Tefnahkt was gone. His robes billowed to the floor along with a pile of ash, a faint, pallid light like glowing wisps of wind-blown rain gently flowing into Ankhu's core.

Djedar scrambled back, trying to rejoin Dunewalker and Buharum. They regrouped in terror, their movements like those of frightened rats under the gaze of one who wielded godlike power. Djedar found himself staring into a deep red glow from the empty, pitiless eye-sockets of the skull of the risen mummy.

Pharaoh Ankhu the Endless, God-King, Demon-Sired, High Priest of the Black Temple and oppressor of Kemhet, rose to his full, inhuman height...

And turned his gaze upon the Medjai.

TO BE CONTINUED

in...

Djedar Rath, Book II: The Curse of Ankhu

Coming 2025

Author Note

Thank you for reading one of my books! I hope you will read this series in its entirety and consider reading other stories in this universe, particularly my primary series set in Wulfgard: *The Prophecy of the Six*.

I have always wanted to tell my stories, and while it has its many hardships, I've finally settled into self-publishing books such as this one. My brother, Justin R. R. Stebbins – who also drew the cover art for this book – and I have worked virtually our whole lives on this universe, and my characters mean everything to me. I'm very happy you found your way here to some of my many stories told in the world of Wulfgard.

While storytelling is my deepest passion, I have an endless fascination with many subjects, including filmmaking, studying history, folklore, mythology, and much more. All of these affect my writing methods as well as the stories I tell and the world in which my characters exist.

For many years, my brother and I have worked to ensure a certain level of historical accuracy and attention to detail in the world of Wulfgard, while also paying close attention to our incorporation of real-world myth and legend alongside our original concepts. Although Wulfgard is not set in the real world, it is very heavily inspired by a different take on history and mythology, combined with original aspects.

I truly hope you enjoyed this book and you will take the time to explore my other and future works. If you like my work, please help spread the word to others who may be interested and leave this book, and my other books you purchase, reviews across the Internet. Every new reader means a lot to me, and in the world of self-publishing, they can be very hard to find! So thank you again for another step toward making my dream come true: sharing my stories and characters with the world.

And remember – this is only the beginning of the tale. Be sure to check out the other novellas in this series!

The stories of all these characters, especially Djedar Rath, will also continue in future Wulfgard works. Keep an eye out for many more novellas, short story collections, novels, and comics, and especially *The Prophecy of the Six* series, and be sure to read the sequel to this book and the second installment in the *Wulfgard: Djedar Rath* series: *The Curse of Ankhu.*

Continue exploring the world of Wulfgard

For more Wulfgard books, comics, and stories, be sure to
visit me and my brother online at:

www.WULFGARD.net
and
www.MAVERICKWEREWOLF.com

Scan this QR code to sign up for my newsletter!
Details at the link.

ALSO AVAILABLE:

WULFGARD: Knightfall
A Novel by Maegan A. Stebbins
Illustrated by Justin R. R. Stebbins

Rage.
Few can match the fury of Sir Tom Drake in battle - not even
a Demon of Wrath. When Tom killed just such a fiend in
single combat, a feat of which most mortals would never
dream, he became the Demon Slayer. To the people of his
beloved city of Illikon, Tom is a hero. But his city swears
fealty to the Achaean Empire, and to them, he is just
another knight.

Enter Sir Scaevius, Left Hand of the Emperor. With war
raging against a barbarian alliance massing to the North,

Scaevius takes command of Illikon's armies and orders Tom on a suicide mission. Tom obeys, but not without protest. Soon, he finds himself fighting not only the barbarians, but his own superiors as well – and something else, something supernatural.

A monster is stalking him: a half man, half beast abomination from legend... a werewolf. It haunts his dreams and even his waking hours, and he starts to suffer blackouts, unsure what is real and what is nightmare. Hated by his superiors, hunted by beasts and assassins, Tom Drake must fight for his home, his life, and even his mind. The events that are about to unfold will change his life, and the world, forever.

A thrilling tale of adventure, dashing heroics, chilling horror, alluring mystery, and both personal duels and epic battles centered around memorable characters, *Knightfall* takes you to the edge of your seat in a wild ride set in a traditional dark age heroic fantasy world, where all myths are true – and monsters from legend seek to devour Men. Meet the sharply characterized cast, discover a new realm at once dark yet not without light and hope, and return to fantasy's roots in the series *The Prophecy of the Six* and the world of Wulfgard.

WULFGARD: Into the North
A Graphic Novel by Justin R. R. Stebbins

In Northrim, a Wanderer stumbles down from the Jagged
Edge after a long journey, and runs into a werewolf. In the
Imperial capital, a young elven thief finds herself caught by
demons and assassins hunting for a set of mysterious
ancient artifacts. In the city of Rimegard, a princess
struggles to hide a terrifying secret. And in the darkness
beneath the world, a clan of dwarves wage war with
demonic dark elves. Soon, all their fates are destined to
intertwine. This volume of comics introduces their stories,
comprising the first four chapters of a much larger tale.

Special Thanks

...to my mother, Mary; my father, Jack; and my amazing brothers, Justin and Ryan; always. Without you, the world of Wulfgard would not have been created.

To all my patrons, as well as the following individuals for their generous support throughout my various creative endeavors.

Ajestice
Alex
Caleb Blanchet
Matthew Blanchet
Jared Buniel
Ryan J.
Jan Lingenfelder
Valerie Lingenfelder
Kyle "Ambad" Smith

Other Works

I am always publishing more books, so be sure to look me up online and follow me on social media for updates!

The following list is up to date as of the year this book was published and should not be taken as current.

Set in the world of Wulfgard

This list is roughly in chronological order. *Knightfall* begins the setting's main series and remains the best starting point. There is no "required reading" unless a work is noted as a sequel.

- *Djedar Rath, Book I: The Tomb of Ankhu*
- *Djedar Rath, Book II: The Curse of Ankhu*
- *The Hunt Never Ends*
- *Tales of Wulfgard, Volume I*
- *The Demon's Fang*
- *The Prophecy of the Six, Book I: Knightfall*

Nonfiction/Academic/Research works

- *The Werewolf: Past and Future – Lycanthropy's Lost History and Modern Devolution*
- *The Book of Were-Wolves* by Sabine Baring-Gould, edited, annotated, and translated by Maegan A. Stebbins
- *Werewolf Folklore Stories: A Collection of Real-World Lycanthropy Tales Throughout History*
- *Werewolf Facts* (coming soon)